THE FERNHURST INHERITANCE

Laura and Robert Faulkner are drifting apart — and is it any wonder, when Robert spends every available moment working? It doesn't help that he is attracted to his business partner, the worldly, glamorous Stella . . . Meanwhile, their son Neil Faulkner, back from a year in America, finds himself falling in love with their houseguest, Susan. Susan, however, has worries of her own to contend with . . .

MARY CUMMINS

THE FERNHURST INHERITANCE

Complete and Unabridged

LINFORD
Leicester

First published in Great Britain in 1986

First Linford Edition
published 2007

British Library CIP Data

Cummins, Mary
    The Fernhurst inheritance.—Large print ed.—
Linford romance library
    1. Love stories
    2. Large type books
    I. Title
    823.9′14 [F]

    ISBN 978–1–84617–985–3

Published by
F. A. Thorpe (Publishing)
Anstey, Leicestershire

Set by Words & Graphics Ltd.
Anstey, Leicestershire
Printed and bound in Great Britain by
T. J. International Ltd., Padstow, Cornwall

This book is printed on acid-free paper

Family Problems

Laura Faulkner stared out of her bedroom window across the well-kept lawns and flowerbeds of the gardens surrounding Fernhurst, the lovely home she had always known. Normally she loved this time of the evening since it gave her an opportunity to relax and change before her husband, Robert, arrived home for dinner.

But at the moment there was a great deal on her mind, and her dressing-table mirror showed a small furrow between her eyes. She bent forward and tried to smooth it a little.

At forty-eight she had few wrinkles to worry about, but she had never thought of herself as being particularly pretty, even in her youth.

However, there was no point in inviting wrinkles, and once again her thoughts went to Robert. Was he disappointed in her, she wondered? Sometimes it seemed she no longer knew how he felt about her, or about their life together, and that frightened her.

The sound of car wheels in the drive disturbed her reverie, and through the opened window she could hear her husband's deep voice and that of their son, Neil. The car door slammed and she was aware of their footsteps as they walked into the house together.

It was lovely to have Neil home again, Laura thought, after the year he'd spent in America. He was a young man of his time and she'd marvelled when, even as a small boy, he'd understood computers and used them with ease. She, on the other hand, felt inadequate when faced with the kind of merchandise which was manufactured by Ross/Faulkner Industries.

She still preferred to work out her own affairs with the aid of a pencil and paper, and had long since given up trying to understand the modern telecommunications equipment so dear to her husband's heart, and now to Neil's.

The business world of her menfolk was one she'd never had any desire to share.

Perhaps that had been a mistake, Laura mused, as she rose to check her appearance in the full-length mirror. She'd brushed out her simply-cut hair and touched her face lightly with powder. Her dress was very plain, but the heavy misty-blue silk showed a lovely figure, slender for her age and very elegant.

The gold necklace she put on had been a twenty-first birthday gift from her father, Roger Kingsley, who had once owned Fernhurst, and Laura wore them constantly.

Despite the necklace and matching earrings, she'd look dull beside Stella Ross, Laura thought ruefully, and tried not to think too deeply about the beautiful woman who had recently inherited the whole of her father's interest in Ross/Faulkner Industries.

Robert wouldn't be human if he didn't sometimes compare the two of them.

She picked up a spray of exotic perfume, then paused before putting it down again. Robert had given it to her, and she remembered how surprised she'd been at the time because it was much more sophisticated than his usual gifts — too sophisticated for her tastes. She'd wondered where he'd got the idea from — and then she'd thought of Stella. Worldly, glamorous Stella.

Well, he couldn't turn her into another Stella with that sort of gift. She could only be herself.

As she left the room she paused beside her bedside table and picked up a letter, glancing again at the stylish handwriting.

Susan Ashley's handwriting was very different from that of her mother, Laura reflected. She'd always imagined Helen's daughter being a small carbon copy of her mother, but now she wondered a little. Then she put it out of her mind as she walked downstairs and into the lounge, placing the letter in her pocket.

Robert Faulkner was talking forcibly to his son, but they both stopped when Laura walked into the room.

'Hello, dear.' Robert smiled. 'There you are. Had a good day?'

'Reasonably good.' Laura nodded, accepting the small sherry Neil poured out for her and sitting down in one of the large armchairs.

It was a rhetorical question, however, because Robert was already back on his original subject.

'Now you're back, Neil, it's time you took your place in the community, and the Hunt Dinner and Dance seems as good a place as any to begin.'

Laura noticed the flash of apprehension cross her son's eyes but his father was oblivious to it.

'You'll meet some nice people,' Robert Faulkner continued, 'and it's good for business. And what else are you doing on Saturday evening anyway?'

'I need time to settle down again,' Neil said, his voice a little strained.

'Well, your mother and I are going. Which reminds me, Laura . . . ' His eyes travelled faintly critically over her. 'Maybe you should buy a new dress. Get the best you can find. It's a present from me.'

'Just a minute, Robert.' Laura held up her hand, frowning a little. 'When is the Hunt Dance?'

'This Saturday. It's OK, I've already accepted for both of us. There's no need for you to do anything except dress up. I forgot to mention it,' he added a little apologetically, 'but if you remember from last year, it's quite a dressy affair . . . '

'I can't go,' Laura said quietly.

Robert stopped in mid-flow and stared at her.

'What do you mean, you can't go?'

Laura looked him firmly in the eyes.

'You should have asked before you accepted for me, Robert, and perhaps you might have remembered that we have a guest arriving on Saturday evening. Helen Ashley's daughter, Susan.'

Robert looked clearly puzzled.

'I spoke to you about her at the time,' Laura reminded him, trying to hide the exasperation she felt. 'You agreed we should invite her to stay for a week or two, so I did and she's due to arrive here on Saturday.'

She took Susan's letter out of her pocket and showed it to him.

'This confirms the arrangements. She has to be picked up from Lockerbie Station.'

'Surely the girl can look after herself . . . ' Robert began, but then he met Laura's cool glance and retreated. 'No, perhaps not,' he added.

'Perhaps I could meet her,' Neil offered, though he was obviously reluctant.

'Thanks, Neil, but I'd still have to be here,' his mother said quietly. 'She's bound to feel strange.'

Robert frowned thoughtfully. 'The

girl's an invalid, isn't she?'

'Oh no, it isn't that bad,' Laura said quickly. 'But she has been unwell and needs to convalesce.'

Laura frowned, remembering Helen's letter. She'd known Helen since school-days and it was very unlike the other woman to give way to her fears and confess to being so worried about her daughter.

'*At first I thought she was merely run-down,*' Helen had written. '*She's a secretary at one of our Local Government offices and she's been working very hard, especially since they started to cut down on the staff. Now she's lost all her energy and has been given leave of absence against her holidays.*

'*But I think there's more to it, Laura,* the letter had gone on. *She'd been seeing a lot of a young man but now he seems to have disappeared from the scene, and I think Susan's taking it badly.*

'*I think she's deeply in love with him*

8

and he's walked out on her. At any rate . . .'

Helen had then described Susan's withdrawn looks and how she felt that a week or two away from London might help her get over the Rex Windham affair.

'*Because I'm sure Rex has hurt her in some way,*' she'd ended. '*Had it been anything else but Rex, she would have confided in me.*'

Laura had consulted Robert over Helen's letter and he'd happily agreed to having the girl at Fernhurst. Then she had written to Susan herself to make the offer. Naturally Laura had given no indication that the girl's mother had confided her true concerns to her; she had said only that her mother had thought she might enjoy a break away from the city.

Now Laura placed the reply from Susan on the coffee table. It was rather a stiff little letter, very polite and very carefully written.

But there had also been gratitude,

and Laura was determined that the girl be made as welcome as possible, although a glance at the faces of her menfolk was enough to tell her that neither of them was looking forward to the prospect of having a stranger in their midst.

Annie McCall, the housekeeper at Fernhurst since the days of Laura's parents, Roger and Evelyn Kingsley, came into the room just then.

'Dinner's ready now, Mrs Faulkner,' she said, then turned as the Faulkners' younger child, Debbie, came rushing through the hall and into the lounge, her tennis racket swinging.

'Guess what!' she cried breathlessly.

'We'll guess nothing, Debbie, when you rush in an hour late for your meal and in need of a good wash,' her father retorted sternly. 'Where have you been?'

'I told you,' Debbie informed him resentfully, 'and I told Annie I'd be late — though it isn't nearly an hour. There was a big match on tonight.'

'Well, you'll have to tell us all about it later. We've waited long enough.'

Debbie hesitated, her face mulish. None of them took any interest in her affairs. All they were interested in at the moment was Neil, and she found all this computer business a dead bore.

No-one shared her passion for tennis, and even her mother appeared to have other things on her mind whenever she tried to talk to her. Debbie wanted to tell them loftily that they could eat dinner without her, but the exercise and concentration which had won her tonight's match against girls much older and more experienced had given her a tremendous appetite.

'I'll be right down, Annie,' she promised. 'I'm starving.'

'Hurry then,' Annie replied, her eyes soft. Debbie was still very much 'her baby,' but she could see trouble ahead if Laura didn't take more interest in the girl.

Really Laura was better at looking after other people's unfortunates, Annie thought wryly, remembering all the instructions she'd been given for preparing Susan Ashley's room.

Debbie rushed away, but her eyes were full of disappointment. How wonderful it would have been if only her family had welcomed her home with praise for her skill and talent.

And she didn't have a great deal of time to waste! She should be training now if she was to win a place in bigger competitions.

As she struggled into a dress, which she hated, her eyes roamed round the picture gallery which Laura had allowed her to re-hang after her room was recently decorated.

There were all the pictures of her idols, Martina Navratilova and Chris Lloyd smiling at her beside an autographed photograph of Virginia Wade. She'd cut Sue Barker's picture from a magazine, and she'd also pinned up pictures of John McEnroe and Boris Becker.

It was her great dream that perhaps

one day she too would join their ranks as a world-class tennis player.

Her coach had tried to talk to her father, but although Robert Faulkner had been delighted to hear of his daughter's success, he'd been unable to take seriously the idea that Debbie might make a career out of her ability to play tennis.

Her examination results in ordinary subjects were also excellent and Robert believed she'd do well at university and take up a professional career.

Tennis was all very well, but it was only a game . . .

It was *not* only a game, Debbie thought rebelliously, as she ran downstairs to the dining-room. It was her life . . .

★   ★   ★

' . . . perhaps Debbie might take her to the tennis club,' her mother was saying as Debbie settled herself at the dinner table.

'Who?' asked Debbie.

'Susan Ashley. You don't listen, dear,' Laura said patiently, thinking that although Debbie complained that they never showed any interest in her affairs, she excluded her family from her thoughts with equal ease.

'My friend Helen's daughter. I told you about her. She hasn't been well for the past few weeks and is coming here for a change of air and a change of scene. I thought perhaps you could help her to enjoy herself.'

Debbie grimaced. She seemed to have been hearing about Susan Ashley half her life.

'But, Mum! She's old!' she exclaimed. 'I'd be . . . I mean, she'd — well,' Debbie hesitated. 'She's more Neil's age.' She looked at her brother for help.

'She's twenty-four,' her mother put in.

'I told you. Two years younger than Neil.'

'Now, wait a minute . . . ' Neil remonstrated. 'I came back home to

14

work harder than I've ever worked in my life. I've no time for social occasions. It's going to take months of effort to establish my own business, but I mean to specialise in supplying memory chips. There's a marvellous market for this in the USA and I know I can make a success of it. I learned exactly what they want while I was over there.'

Robert Faulkner was nodding in agreement, but Laura's eyes were troubled. She wasn't a businesswoman but she did have some sound common sense, and she kept in touch with world affairs.

'Won't it have to be heavily financed?' she asked.

'That's a problem which can be overcome,' Robert told her. 'And if I may say so, Laura, my dear, it's our problem, Neil's and mine. We know what we can and can't do in business.'

Laura bit her lip, feeling snubbed. So much for trying to take a more active interest in Robert's affairs! It seemed a long time since he'd talked over his hopes and dreams for the future with her, yet at one time they had shared it all . . .

★ ★ ★

After dinner the family retired to the sitting-room, though Debbie excused herself soon afterwards to do some homework in her room and Laura found herself left to read a book or to take up her embroidery while Robert and Neil were engrossed in conversation about business affairs.

She felt restless and discontented, a feeling that was in no way dispelled when Robert finally suggested it was time for bed.

Going upstairs together was a time-honoured ritual. It was rare for Laura to go to bed on her own, and she liked to wait up for Robert even if he were late home from an executive meeting.

As she brushed out her hair, she watched him removing his shoes and wrinkling his toes with satisfaction. But when his eyes met hers in the dressing-table mirror, she could see he was far from content.

'I wish you could make other arrangements for this girl,' he said rather irritably.

'Her name is Susan. Susan Ashley,' Laura reminded him. 'You should know her name by now, Robert. I've talked about her a lot and you know that Helen is my oldest friend.'

'I should know that by now, too,' he told her. 'Look, I agree that you did consult me about inviting her — sorry, Susan — here, but I didn't know her arrival would coincide with the Hunt Dinner.' He gazed at her reproachfully. 'I don't want to miss that, but you know I need a partner.'

Laura avoided his eyes as she continued to prepare for bed and Robert sighed heavily before disappearing round the door towards the bathroom.

Why was she standing out against

him like this, she wondered as she slipped between the sheets. There had been a time when she would simply have arranged for Annie McCall to look after Susan for an hour or two.

She lay in bed gazing up at the ceiling.

Several things were niggling at her, in fact, and she hardly knew which was the more important.

For one thing, there had been an odd little note of appeal in Susan's letter which she couldn't ignore, even though it made her feel uneasy. The girl was eager enough to accept the invitation, yet a few years ago, when she had met Susan while visiting Helen in London and had suggested a similar break, the girl had seemed reluctant, and had been too young to disguise her relief when Helen had reminded her she had several commitments to fulfil in the city.

Fernhurst must seem like the back of beyond to someone with Susan's background, Laura mused, yet now she seemed eager to come despite the stilted nature of the letter.

Laura had the odd idea that a lifeline had been grasped, but quite how she could help she didn't really know. All she could do was offer support.

But that wasn't the only thing on her mind.

She hadn't cared for the fact that Robert had accepted the Hunt Dance invitation for both of them. There had been a great deal too much of that lately, and she was beginning to resent his making these decisions for her. She was a person in her own right and she felt he was taking her far too much for granted. She deserved the courtesy of at least being asked.

Her thoughts were broken when Robert returned from the bathroom. She noticed the grim set of his mouth.

'If you won't come . . . ' he began.

'Not 'won't' — can't,' she amended.

'All right, can't . . . though I think a solution could be found for Susan if only you applied your mind to it.' He looked at her pleadingly. 'Surely you must realise it's essential for me to go to the Hunt Dinner and Dance, and with a partner. I might be chairman of the finance company next year, and you know there are several people on the Hunt committee who would be more than helpful to me and to Neil.'

But he could see that her mind was made up and he sighed.

'Look, if you can't come, I'll be forced to ask Stella Ross.'

The name seemed to hang between them. Laura couldn't guess how Robert felt about the beautiful woman who was now his partner in the firm.

Surely Stella was the type of woman Robert should have married, she thought jealously.

She watched him pick up a book and leaf idly through the pages before putting it down again. Then he removed his dressing-gown and slipped into bed.

'You can read if you like,' he told her. 'I'm tired. I think I'll just settle down.'

He was often tired at night, Laura

thought unhappily, as she flicked over the pages of her magazine.

Finally she put it on her bedside table and switched off her own bedside light.

Robert was pretending to be asleep, but she knew by the taut way in which he held his body that he was still very much awake.

She was so much aware of him and so often she longed for the passionate love that there had once been between them.

She still loved him in that way, but she sensed that his desire for her had changed. It was true he still loved her in his own way, but the fire had gone. He only needed her love occasionally, and while she accepted this, her pride forced her to withhold the fierce nature of her own passion.

She tried to push such thoughts away. She must believe that Robert loved her, and that Stella wasn't winning a place in his affections.

Surely he'd loved her when they first married, she assured herself. But the treacherous thought came that he had only married her because of Fernhurst. It had been in the family for over two hundred years before it had been sold to him, and he had a fine sense of continuity.

Full of pride, he'd show people round telling them that it had been in 'our' family since the time of the first Jacobite Rebellion. Would he still have married her if she hadn't been Laura Kingsley?

She never pursued such thoughts without feeling a deep sense of failure . . .

Slowly, in spite of her thoughts, Laura drifted off to sleep, unlike Robert, who remained awake for some time.

Laura was changing towards him, he felt, and his eyes were bleak as he gazed at the shaft of moonlight which shone between the curtains. He could feel it, sense it in the way she spoke to him and in her eyes as she looked at him.

He sighed. He had no choice but to

ask Stella Ross to the Hunt Dinner and Dance. A great many local businessmen had been invited and everyone knew that Stella had inherited all her father's holdings in Ross/Faulkner Industries.

There would be no eyebrows raised if he asked Stella to partner him to the dinner. Nor would she make any bones about accepting. Stella knew very well the value of such social occasions.

In fact, he mused, Stella knew the value of most things to the last penny. He'd never encountered a woman like her before.

Why couldn't Laura put more effort into being his wife? She was so cool and withdrawn on these occasions and only Robert could see that she was in an agony of shyness at times. Yet her background should give her every confidence in herself, and hadn't he himself once told her that shyness was a form of conceit?

Gradually, though, she'd have opted out of going anywhere with him unless he managed to persuade her otherwise.

He'd taken to accepting invitations for both of them, knowing that he could soon arrange for her to be with him, but now Laura was beginning to rebel against this.

Perhaps she was right. He should always ask her first.

Sometimes she could make him feel so brash when she gave him one of her cool looks, and he'd remember that it was Laura's family who truly belonged at Fernhurst.

Even her children belonged by right of birth. It was only he, Robert Faulkner, who had bought his way into the place. Yet he probably loved it as much as any of them. The effort he'd put into creating the gardens and renovating the house had been done for love of the place.

Yet he could never be sure how Laura felt about this.

Sadly, he mused that he couldn't talk to her about things any more. He wasn't even sure if she still loved him, and his uncertainty made him clumsy and awkward with her.

Tomorrow, however, he decided, he'd ask Stella Ross to partner him to the Hunt Dinner and Laura could make his apologies to their latest guest. She was a London girl and no doubt sophisticated enough to understand, being well used to a busy social life.

Laura shouldn't make such a fuss. It could all have been resolved quietly and without fuss . . . if only she cared enough!

Running Away...

Susan Ashley woke feeling as if she was to face yet another day in a dark tunnel filled with depression. She'd no need to look in the mirror to know that her face was pale with dark rings around her eyes.

When she was fully awake, she remembered that it wasn't just an ordinary day. Soon she would be catching a train for Lockerbie in Scotland where she would stay with the Faulkners at Fernhurst.

Downstairs she could hear her mother bustling about in the kitchen, delighted that Susan had accepted Laura Faulkner's invitation and no doubt fussily preparing a breakfast which her daughter would be unable to eat.

It was because she felt so tired that Susan had decided to take a later train so that she wouldn't have to hurry to the station. Everything was such an effort these days.

In ordinary circumstances she would never have dreamed of accepting this invitation from Laura Faulkner, knowing that her mother had probably asked for her to be invited. That embarrassed her since she knew her mother wouldn't have found it an easy request to make.

She remembered Mrs Faulkner as a tall, slim, cool-looking woman, very different from her own mother who was now comfortably plump with the same blonde wavy hair as Susan had inherited. Her mother and Laura had been close friends at school and they'd kept up their friendship over the years, even though they saw little of one another these days.

'I wouldn't have thought you'd have much in common,' Susan had remarked at one time.

'Perhaps not,' her mother had replied, 'but she was always so steadfast, and I always knew where I was with her. And

I was very fond of her — well, I still am. I think she needs people to love her.' Helen had gazed at her thoughtfully. 'You mustn't judge by appearances, dear. Laura and I can always count on one another for help, if we really need it . . . not that I ever have needed it,' she'd added hastily, with a sideways glance at her daughter.

It had been easy for Susan to guess even before that remark that her mother must have turned to Laura Faulkner for help with regard to herself. When she had become ill and had to get leave of absence from work, she hadn't even been able to summon up enough energy to pretend that nothing was wrong, or that Rex wasn't to blame.

At the thought of Rex Windham, Susan's eyes darkened. But a moment later Helen Ashley was tapping lightly on the bedroom door and carrying her breakfast in on a tray.

'It's a lovely day for your journey, darling,' she said cheerfully. 'We needn't leave for the station for ages yet, so I thought you'd enjoy a nice leisurely breakfast in bed. There's fruit juice, bacon and egg and toast. Marmalade, too — and I'll just go and fetch the coffee now.'

'Oh, Mum!'

Susan sat up, ready to protest against the bacon and egg, but already her mother had gone, hurrying downstairs to pick up the pot of coffee and the cream jug.

Susan loved her parents and appreciated her mother's tender care, but it only made her feel worse. It was one reason why she had pocketed her pride and accepted this invitation to Scotland. At least she would be free of her mother's anxious eyes, her probing questions and the disapproval on her face whenever Rex Windham was mentioned.

It was so difficult to keep the truth from her, yet if she knew everything, how much worse it would be.

'You'll love Scotland, dear,' Mrs

Ashley said happily as she reappeared with the coffee pot. 'I used to go to Fernhurst years ago when Laura and I were at school together. Her mother was such a charming lady — a little like Laura, really, though she has a lot of her father in her, too.

'Mrs Kingsley died while Laura was still at school, and I think she was glad of me as a friend at that time. Later she looked after Fernhurst for her father, but his investments were poor — or something of the kind. At any rate, there were money problems and the estate had to be sold to Robert Faulkner. Poor Mr Kingsley didn't live long after that.'

Susan drank a cup of coffee and allowed her mother to rattle on, giving her information about the Faulkners, though she was scarcely listening.

She had little interest in the Faulkners. She remembered there was a boy, Neil, only a year or two older than herself. As a schoolboy he'd been insufferable, full of his own importance, and she'd disliked him intensely.

What sort of man was he now, she wondered idly. She would make a point of avoiding him, and his father, whom she remembered as a tall, energetic man who always seemed to have a briefcase under his arm.

There was a small girl, too, who had clamoured for attention. She'd be a young teenager now . . .

'Susan, dear, you must try to eat your bacon and egg,' Mrs Ashley admonished gently.

Susan grimaced. 'You know I never eat breakfast, Mum.'

'But it's such a long journey, and there's no guarantee that you'll get anything to eat on the train . . . '

'Mum!' Susan fought down her nerves and smiled into her mother's anxious eyes. 'I'm twenty-four years old. I can look after myself . . . '

'But you've been ill!' Mrs Ashley protested. 'And these viruses are very hard to get over. You must take it easy.' She sighed. 'I wish you'd let me take you to that specialist Mrs Jardine recommended.'

'No, Mum!'

Susan's voice was sharper than she would have wished. If only her mother wouldn't fuss so much!

'It's Rex Windham, isn't it?' Helen Ashley asked, looking at her with concern. 'You might as well be honest with me, Susan, now you're going away for a week or two.' She regarded her daughter with anxious eyes. If only she would open up to her more. 'Has he let you down?' she asked softly, insistently. 'I know you were in love with him, but if he doesn't appreciate your love, then it's his loss. You'll find some other nice man,' she added gently.

'I don't want any other 'nice man',' Susan declared, her voice choking with tears, 'and I don't want to talk about Rex.'

Mrs Ashley could sense the strain in her daughter's voice and her heart ached to help, but she knew there was nothing more she could do.

'All right, dear,' she said, 'but I'll be very disappointed if you don't come back home with roses in your cheeks . . . '

And with Rex Windham consigned to the past, she thought silently, as she carried the breakfast tray to the kitchen.

Yet he had been such a pleasant young man, and quite an expert in the world of antiques. She remembered how he had told her quite a lot about a few pieces of old blue and white pottery, advising her to take good care of it and not to sell it without asking his advice.

'There are sharks about, Mrs Ashley,' he'd warned, smiling a little. 'You've got to know what you're doing.'

He'd pointed out everything he considered of special value in the house and she had been delighted by his interest. Even James, her husband, had liked him, which was quite unusual as he was very protective of his only daughter.

But there was no need for Rex to

have disappeared out of Susan's life without making a proper break with her, Helen thought irritably.

She only hoped that this trip to Scotland would do the girl — indeed, them both — some good, for the past few weeks had been tense for her as well as for Susan. She knew that her daughter had been making efforts to contact Rex, ringing up his flat and his place of work, but if Susan had chosen not to confide in her — well, she couldn't say anything to her until she did.

Helen didn't blame Rex if he was no longer in love with the girl, but she blamed him for sliding out of her life without telling her, honestly, how he felt. Susan would have faced that with dignity.

As it was, she'd been left waiting and wondering, and that angered Helen Ashley very much.

★　★　★

Susan had deliberately put all thoughts of Rex Windham behind her until she was comfortably settled on the train bound for Scotland. She had accepted a bundle of magazines and a bag of fruit from her mother and they'd clung to one another fiercely.

'I'll be OK, Mum,' Susan had told her huskily. 'Don't worry about me.'

Now she laid the magazines aside and leaned back in her seat, and almost immediately the memory of Rex's thin, dark face was before her.

She couldn't believe what one of his colleagues from Mortimer Antiques had told her. It couldn't be true! Rex wasn't a thief!

Yet apparently the evidence against him was very strong. One or two items of stock had been removed, Charles Fuller, Rex's colleague, had told her, and it could only be Rex who had taken them. He was now suspended pending an investigation, and when Susan had tried to reach him at his flat, she'd found it locked up. Nor had he left any message for her.

As the days passed and she received no message, Susan had begun to grow desperate and had forgotten to be discreet when ringing from home. She'd tried every friend she'd ever heard Rex mention. Too late she'd realised that her mother had witnessed her frantic efforts to find him.

Where was he? He couldn't just walk out on her like that . . . he just couldn't, she thought, as the familiar headache began to press upon her. The decision to come away from London for a week or two hadn't been easy, but she'd begun to realise it was the only thing she could do.

She needed time to think. She needed to be by herself for a little while.

★   ★   ★

Neil's offer to meet Susan had been accepted gratefully by his mother since he flatly refused to attend the Hunt

Dinner and Dance. His father was taking Stella Ross as his partner, but although there were several girls in their crowd who would have been happy to partner Neil, he wasn't interested.

As he strode up and down the station platform, Neil's thoughts were full of his new project and the ideas which had taken root while he was in America. He'd spent a year in Silicon Valley, the most exciting year of his life. What marvels could be wrought with new technology and how wide open the field was for supplying the 'memory' chips he so much wanted to make.

At least his father hadn't required too much persuasion to see his point of view, but his mother might be a different matter.

'We'll need heavy finance,' Robert Faulkner had mused. 'And the banks are being cagey at the moment unless we have excellent collateral.'

'That's out as far as I'm concerned,' Neil had said despondently. 'I couldn't raise anything like the amount needed.

The trouble is, we wouldn't employ that many people and I doubt if we'd qualify for a government grant.'

There had been silence between them for a moment, then Robert had looked up.

'I have something of value,' he'd said.

Neil had looked at him, his interest roused.

'I couldn't raise very much on my own business ventures because Stella would block me all the way — but we have got Fernhurst.'

'Fernhurst!' Neil had stared at him in astonishment. 'We couldn't touch Fernhurst. What would Mum say?'

Robert had pursed his lips.

'I hold the deeds. It could be done without her knowledge — but I would have to rely on your discretion.'

He'd looked his son straight in the eye, but Neil's thoughts had been in turmoil.

'But — Fernhurst! It's Mum's home!' he'd protested.

'And yours . . . and Debbie's,' Robert

had said rather dryly. 'You're all Kingsleys. But if your figures are at all accurate, then there would be no question of losing Fernhurst. In fact, it would put it on a more secure footing.'

Neil had regarded him speculatively and Robert had run a hand through his hair.

'Look,' he'd begun, 'it costs money to keep a house like this up, Neil — Fernhurst eats up a lot of money. We need new ideas, new ventures. That's why you went to America. Now we must risk something to reap the benefit of all your new knowledge.'

Neil had nodded, knowing his father was in earnest, and then they'd had to drop the subject when his mother had joined them.

She must never know, Neil now thought, though he felt both excited and vaguely apprehensive. The prospect of this new venture made the palms of his hands sweat. He knew he would never have settled down to enjoy the Hunt Dinner with all this excitement fresh in his mind, especially if he'd had to entertain some young lady. He liked girls and enjoyed their company, but his whole soul was given over to the job he had to do. He had no alternative now.

Neil pulled himself out of his thoughts as the train approached.

He stood back from the platform as it slid smoothly into the station and a few passengers alighted and began to make their way to the exit.

There was only one girl on her own, and Neil experienced a slight sense of shock as he went forward to meet her. She was tall and slender with a face of such unusual beauty that he could only stare at her silently for a moment.

Then his good manners surfaced and he held out his hand.

'Miss Ashley . . . Susan?' he asked. 'It's been a long time, hasn't it?'

'Neil? It is Neil, isn't it?' she asked. 'Yes, it has been a long time.'

Susan was so tired by the journey and her own unhappy thoughts that she could only stare dully at him.

He'd grown very tall and his rugged features showed strength of character. She'd have to get to know him all over again, but he certainly had more warmth and friendliness than she remembered, and for that she was grateful.

'Did you have a good journey?' he was asking.

'We were held up here and there, but we made up the time between stations,' she told him, and Neil could sense the fatigue and strain in her voice as she spoke.

Susan Ashley certainly didn't look well, and he'd never seen such misery and anxiety in a girl's eyes.

'You look tired, Susan,' he remarked, now that he'd been able to look at her more closely. 'But never mind, the car's waiting outside so I'll get you home as quickly as I can,' he added cheerfully, reaching to take her bag from her.

Susan flushed and once again the remembrance of her worries caused her eyes to dull with pain. Was her unhappiness so obvious? She'd have to pull herself together before she met the rest of the Faulkner family, or they might start to ask awkward questions.

She bit her lip anxiously as she strode out of the station beside Neil. She'd wanted to come to Fernhurst to get away from everything, but there were some things you couldn't run away from. She knew they'd remain with her wherever she went, and she'd have to try to conceal such anxieties.

For the first time she realised just how difficult that might be and wondered if she'd perhaps made a mistake in accepting Laura Faulkner's invitation. Was it really the . . . ?

'I . . . I beg your pardon?' Suddenly she became aware that Neil was talking to her. She looked up to find him regarding her anxiously, having stored her case in the car boot.

'I only wanted to know if you'll be OK in the front seat, or perhaps you'd rather lie down in the back?' He hesitated slightly. 'My mother said you'd been ill.'

Susan's heart sank. What kind of impression must the Faulkner family have of her?

'Oh, no need to fuss,' she said with a quick smile. 'I'm just a bit wilted after the journey. I'll be fine in the front.'

'Good,' Neil said cheerfully, obviously brightening, much to her relief. 'I've brought a flask of coffee. Would you like some?'

'Oh, yes, please. I didn't have anything on the train.'

Watching Susan as she drank her coffee, he noticed how frail she looked in spite of her beauty, and something stirred in his heart. She'd been through a bad time, and he decided then and there to do everything possible to make her stay with his family a happy one.

He hadn't wanted her to come because he already had a great deal on his mind and would have even more in the future if he were to establish the business which was so dear to his heart. But surely, he thought to himself, he could spare time for this lovely girl? She looked like a bruised blossom and he felt strangely sensitive to her plight.

'What are you doing these days, Neil?' Susan asked with forced cheerfulness as they finished their coffee and he turned the key in the ignition.

'Well . . . ' He glanced at her as he steered the car into the main road. Was she really interested, or merely being polite? Well, at least she was trying to take an interest.

'I'm into computers,' he told her. 'Memory chips, for example.' Then, noticing her interested glance, he went on more eagerly, 'Actually I've just come back from a year in the States with some ideas for what's needed in today's market. To cut a long story short, I want to start my own business.'

She asked him some more questions and soon he almost seemed to have forgotten her as he was caught up in his own enthusiasm.

His eager voice sounded soothingly in Susan's ears as she tried to follow what he was saying, but eventually the movement of the car made her sleepy so she was almost startled when he finally drove up to the front door of Fernhurst.

★ ★ ★

'Well, we're home,' he said proudly.

'It's a lovely old house,' Susan said, looking up at the stone frontage and trying to hide her tiredness. It was, perhaps, a little older than she had expected but its very age gave it an air of security.

She climbed out of the car, and Laura Faulkner ran down the steps to welcome her with a warm hug.

'You must be tired, my dear,' she said. 'Hungry, too.'

'Not terribly hungry,' Susan said.

'Oh, but we kept supper for when you arrived,' Debbie informed her, stepping forward to shake hands.

'Debbie!' her mother said warningly, then turned once more to Susan. 'We aren't sticklers for time here,' she assured her. 'You must suit yourself about meals.' She smiled warmly. 'We want you to feel at home as much as possible.'

'Thank you, Mrs Faulkner,' Susan replied awkwardly.

'You used to call me 'Aunt Laura',' Laura put in with a kind smile.

'Aunt Laura,' Susan repeated obediently, although she felt no warmth but instead was slightly in awe of her hostess who looked every bit as cool and elegant as she remembered.

Laura ushered Susan into the nice, comfortable sitting-room. Susan found it shabbier than she might have expected, but decided she liked it that way.

Neil disappeared upstairs with her case, while Laura invited her to sit down for a bit to catch her breath after the journey.

Laura's eyes were anxious as she

surveyed Susan. Helen certainly hadn't exaggerated when she'd said the girl had been unwell. She looked like she was going to need a lot of care and attention, and Laura was glad she'd decided to stay at home to welcome her.

'Now I'll take you up to your room so that you can freshen up before supper,' she began. 'Unless, of course, you'd prefer to go straight to bed and have a tray in your room?'

'Oh no, thank you,' Susan protested quickly. 'I'm perfectly all right.'

It was starting already, she thought with dismay. It wasn't going to be any better than living at home.

'I'll show you to your room,' Debbie offered, and her mother smiled her appreciation, thinking that perhaps Susan would be very good for her daughter.

The room Susan had been given was bright and airy, decorated in restful shades of green and cream, and overlooking the front lawn.

As Debbie showed her around it occurred to Susan that she hadn't yet met Mr Faulkner. She waited until Debbie had shown her the bathroom next door and the whereabouts of her own bedroom, before enquiring politely after him.

'He's attending a dinner,' Debbie told her airily. 'Mum couldn't go because you were coming, and he needed to take a partner, so he's taken Stella Ross.'

'Oh.' Slow colour mounted Susan's cheeks. So her visit might have caused some disruption in the household. 'Don't . . . don't you like to go to such functions, Debbie?' she asked.

Who was Stella Ross, she was wondering, and wouldn't it be more natural that Mr Faulkner should ask his daughter to take her mother's place?

'Nobody's ever interested in what I want to do,' Debbie told her bitterly, letting her polite façade drop for a moment. But then, 'Please, forget I said that,' she added quickly, remembering herself. She looked a little awkward. 'Anyway, Stella Ross is Daddy's business partner so it's better that she goes really.'

'I see,' Susan said. Her eyes were searching as she brushed her hair and turned to look at Debbie. Was the girl merely a restless teenager, or had she detected more in Debbie's voice when she had said that nobody would be interested?

'If you're ready, we'll go down,' Debbie said, and Susan followed her silently.

* * *

To her surprise, Susan enjoyed her supper very much. Laura had made her a light, fluffy omelette followed by chocolate mousse, which she found just enough after the journey.

The meal made her feel a great deal better, but she was encouraged to go to bed early and in all honesty could think of nothing she would prefer.

The bed was warm and comfortable and Laura came to settle her down and see that she had everything she needed. Neil, too, had been very solicitous, which had not escaped his mother's bemused eye.

The house was quiet and peaceful, but even so, it was a long time before Susan fell asleep.

She heard the arrival of a car in the early hours of the morning and, some time later, low voices coming up the stairs and passing her room quietly. She assumed it was Mr and Mrs Faulkner, Laura having waited up for her husband.

Despite her welcome, Susan felt it wasn't an easy household. She could sense tension in Laura, and Debbie had a constant air of restless dissatisfaction. Why, wondered Susan. She seemed a bit young to be having boyfriend trouble.

Neil had been charming and attentive, but even so, it was Rex who occupied her mind as she dropped off to sleep. If only she knew where he was. If only she could forget, even for a little while . . .

⋆　⋆　⋆

Laura found Robert pretty uncommunicative as they went upstairs to bed after he arrived home from the Hunt dinner, and she wondered if he was still harbouring his resentment that she hadn't fallen in with his plans.

In fact, however, it was Stella Ross who was occupying his mind. He hadn't expected particularly to enjoy an evening in her company, but, surprisingly, he'd found her an entertaining partner.

Stella had sold her father's old house and bought a small, modern bungalow in Melburgh. Robert hadn't liked it when he'd first seen it, but its modern décor was growing on him. He was beginning to like the fresh, clean lines of the Swedish furniture, and the bright, colourful rugs and cushions which Stella had chosen with a natural artistic flair.

She was a small, slender woman in her early forties, with short, dark hair, beautifully cut to her neat head, and diamond-bright eyes which could sparkle with anger as readily as humour. She reminded Robert of a dragon-fly. He sometimes thought there was a bit of the dragon in her.

'Fly, too,' he'd quipped to Neil after an argumentative session with her over some business matter. She was certainly nobody's fool and he had to be constantly on his toes when they worked together.

That evening he'd collected her from her house, and had been quite taken aback when she came to the door.

Her dress was made of rich, ruby-coloured silk, cut to flatter her excellent figure. She never tried to appear taller than she was, believing that 'petite' was quite an attraction in itself.

Her matching shoes were mere straps to show off her dainty feet. Around her neck she wore a ruby pendant, with matching drop earrings, which had belonged to her mother.

Normally she wore little make-up, but tonight she was made up with subtlety and artistry, and the overall effect of her appearance was stunning.

'I should have brought flowers,' Robert had said as he'd regarded her admiringly. 'Laura should take me to task now and again.'

But even as he was admiring Stella as a very attractive woman, he was acknowledging the fact that the effort she had put into her appearance demonstrated that she appreciated the importance of the occasion in a way that Laura never had with any of the social functions they'd attended together.

'No need for flowers,' Stella had informed him briskly, smiling. 'We're business partners, even for this evening, Robert. But there's no harm in our associates seeing us enjoying ourselves for once! Besides, I do love the chance to dress up once in a while!' She'd smiled at him, then twirled round. 'What do you think of my dress?'

'It's a knock-out,' he'd said sincerely. If only Laura would dress up like Stella, he'd mused . . .

'So it should be for the price it cost me!' she'd told him, laughing. Then she'd taken his arm in a spontaneous gesture. 'Come on, then,' she'd said eagerly, 'let's get going and join the fray.'

Yes, it had been an enjoyable evening, Robert thought now as he got ready for bed. He and Stella had made a few good contacts. In fact, she was even more in tune with his mind socially than she was in business. It seemed they only had to catch one another's eyes to know what the other was thinking.

He was so lost in his own thoughts that he was hardly aware of Laura speaking to him.

'Poor Susan looked worn out,' she was saying, 'Neil thought so, too.'

'Hm?' He dragged his thoughts back

to the present. 'Oh, yes — Susan.' Suddenly he remembered about the girl's arrival. 'Sorry to hear about that,' he added absently, and Laura knew he was hardly listening.

They never seemed to be able to talk to one another these days. Had she made a mistake in stepping aside and allowing Stella Ross to slip into her place?

★ ★ ★

In her modern house, Stella's heels clicked as she climbed the mahogany stairs. Robert Faulkner had been good company that evening and not nearly such a bully as he could be at a directors' meeting, when no idea was worth anything unless he'd brought it up himself! She had to keep her wits about her to maintain her rightful place in the organisation.

But was it worth all the hard work, she wondered. Wasn't Laura Faulkner a happier woman than she was, with only

Fernhurst to run, and her loving family round her?

Stella sighed deeply, a spasm of envy tugging at her heart. She had been in love once, devastatingly, during her teens, but Timothy Hartley had broken off their engagement when he had fallen wildly in love with another girl.

For a while Stella had felt that her life was over, but then her father had taken her in hand and sent her to London, giving her a fine business training.

When he'd died just a few months ago, Stella had been able to step into his shoes with confidence, determined to take her rightful place in the firm. She had become used to meeting men as equals, which was how she regarded Robert Faulkner.

Tonight they had worked very well as a team, Stella thought — and he was a very attractive man. She sincerely hoped that Laura Faulkner appreciated him.

Neil Befriends Susan

Over the next few days Susan did her best to remain in the background at Fernhurst, unaware of the concern that this aroused in Laura.

She had reluctantly left the girl to her own devices while she attended to her various committee duties, but now she thought that there were few girls of Susan's age so withdrawn. All she seemed to do was absorb herself in the London papers and go for short walks. She tended to avoid the family, especially Robert, who had said little to her but whose shrewd eyes had missed nothing.

'Ask Dr Grant to have a look at her,' he'd advised Laura. 'In my opinion, she could do with a check-up.'

But Laura hesitated over taking this advice. After all, Susan wasn't a child and was perfectly capable of consulting a doctor on her own behalf if she felt she needed one.

Instead she had a word with Neil, who was just back from another of his business trips.

'Couldn't you try to take her out of herself, Neil?' she asked anxiously.

Neil had been working very hard, but his next important meeting wasn't for several days and its outcome would depend on the size of the loan his father was arranging for him.

Sometimes Neil felt supremely confident and able to handle his own business, but now and again a small uncertainty would creep in, much to his father's annoyance.

'You must never even think of failure if you're going to be a success,' he'd told him fiercely, and Neil had hurriedly agreed.

However, he had been even more worried than usual just lately, owing to the fact that Fernhurst might have to be put up as collateral. Indeed, the papers were already being prepared.

Now, though, he decided that he would ease up a little and give himself a break — and please his mother by taking Susan out somewhere.

Few girls refused Neil when he asked them out, so he was taken aback when Susan showed no desire for his company and politely declined.

'Surely you could do with a break?' he reasoned. 'We could go somewhere for a drink, or dancing at a club in town. Or if you're still tired, we could go and see a film.'

'I'm not tired,' she informed him briefly.

It was true. The walks and the good food had soon given her back her strength. The trouble was, now she could hardly bear to sit still. She had wanted to phone Rex, and had managed to locate a public call-box, but although she'd left several messages with friends, even daring to give them the address and telephone number of Fernhurst, she hadn't heard from him.

Every morning she hoped the post

would bring a letter, and she'd even scanned the daily papers to see if any mention had been made about his having been accused of stealing from Mortimer's. It was a big enough firm to rate the attention of the Press.

But there had been nothing, and she was finding it just as difficult to live without news of him at Fernhurst as she'd found it in London.

If only she could get away and be on her own where she could do exactly what she liked without upsetting anyone!

But where could she go? She didn't have enough money to rent anywhere, and she realised that such a move would only make everyone worry about her even more.

Besides, Aunt Laura's family had all been so good and patient with her — she couldn't offend them by rejecting their kindness like that.

The one fly in the ointment was the way Robert Faulkner had stared at her when they had first met. She had found it disconcerting for it almost seemed he could read her mind. He knew there was more to her worries than her recent illness . . .

Neil broke into her thoughts.

'If you aren't tired, I think we'll go clubbing,' he said, with a touch of his father's determination in his eyes. He wasn't going to be so easily put off.

Susan sighed. 'I haven't brought anything to wear for something like that.'

Suddenly he was laughing and Susan looked at him with surprise.

'Now I know you're feeling better,' he chortled. 'Even Debbie says that sometimes!'

Susan glanced at him teasingly; his laughter was infectious.

'So she does go out! Yet I don't see any of you coaxing her into dressing up,' she remarked.

'Oh, she's too young for any high life,' Neil informed her. 'Besides, she finds her own amusements.'

His laughter seemed to make her feel

brighter and she decided to go out to the nightclub with him after all.

'But I really don't have anything to wear,' she reminded him.

'You don't have to dress up. Jeans'll do,' he assured her.

'Well, perhaps I can do better than that,' she teased, and Neil was gratified to notice the playful sparkle in her eyes.

She found a swirling, cream-coloured skirt with a simple little top which emphasised her lovely colouring, and once again Neil's eyes were full of admiration as they rested on her. She was, without doubt, the loveliest girl he'd ever seen.

★ ★ ★

Susan made a determined effort to enjoy herself at the club. She found that when she danced with him, their steps matched perfectly, and for a while she was content to partner him, discovering that they liked the same music and responded to the same rhythm.

For Neil it was a night of enchantment as he held the lovely girl in his arms. She was quite different from any girl he had ever known and her body felt warm and soft in his arms. Her shiny, blonde hair made him think of summer days, and he could smell some sort of elusive perfume which was all her own.

Then, suddenly, she was pulling away from him as unconsciously he held her closer. She looked up at him and he could see that the haunted expression was back in her eyes.

'I'd like to go home,' she said unsteadily. 'I've had enough.'

Neil's heart fell.

'But, Susan!' he protested. 'It's early yet. Wouldn't you like a drink at the bar?'

But he could see that all her defences were up again.

'No, thanks. Nothing,' she replied almost coolly. 'I — I just don't want to dance any more.'

He had little option but to concede.

'Can you tell me what it's all about?' he asked gently as they drove home.

Her behaviour both puzzled and worried him. How could he ever help her if he was going to be continually, unconsciously standing on her toes?

But Susan wasn't going to open up.

'I don't know what you mean,' she said tonelessly.

'Oh yes you do,' he said firmly. He knew he couldn't leave it there. 'It's these sudden — changes of mood. That's what I'm talking about.'

He drew into the side of the quiet road and turned to face her, sliding an arm protectively round her shoulders.

'Is there anything upsetting you, Susan, because if I can help . . . '

'Nothing's upsetting me,' she protested quickly, not looking at him but gazing down at her hands.

For a moment he thought he might persist, but then, looking at her closed face and feeling her shoulders tense under his grasp, he knew it was pointless. She was making it very clear that whatever was wrong was none of his business.

With a sigh he turned away and started up the car . . .

* * *

It seemed Laura Faulkner was to spend yet another evening on her own, except for Debbie who was sulking in her room. Evenings alone were becoming increasingly common, she mused sadly as she glanced at the clock, wondering when Robert would be home.

Neil had taken Susan to the theatre, though she'd gone reluctantly after a scene with Debbie who had arrived home after school in a very bad mood.

'What's up with you? Has the tennis tournament been cancelled or something?' her mother had asked.

'No. I played, if you must know . . . '

'Then what's wrong?' Laura had probed. Normally Debbie was full of satisfaction after a tennis match.

'I lost.'

The girl's voice had been full of pain and hurt, and for a moment Laura had felt bewildered, but then she had decided that her daughter must simply be a very poor loser, and would have taken her to task if Susan hadn't been standing in the doorway.

'Don't you see?' Debbie had demanded. 'I . . . sometimes I can't do it by myself. I need . . . ' She'd stopped then, tears of frustration in her eyes that she couldn't articulate how she was feeling.

'Encouragement?' Susan had put in quietly, coming forward, her eyes full of concern.

However, by then Debbie had been too upset to be placated.

'Oh, none of you understand,' she'd muttered briefly and run from the room.

After a moment's awkward silence, Susan had ventured: 'I think she means she needs her family to encourage her.'

'But we do,' Laura had insisted although she'd been strangely disturbed by the scene. 'She's always been encouraged to play good tennis. Why, we've even hired a coach for her!' She'd shaken her head. 'I just don't understand the girl.'

Susan hadn't felt qualified to explain.

Neil had looked in then, cajoling her to go to the theatre with him, and after a while it had seemed easier to say she would than to argue with him. Besides, she was beginning to enjoy going out with him — though he'd landed himself in trouble with his father one time when he'd forgotten to keep an appointment and instead had taken her to Edinburgh for the day.

Robert Faulkner had kept the appointment on his behalf, but it hadn't sat well with him and he hadn't hesitated in making his views on it clear both to Neil and to Laura.

'How long is Susan staying?' he'd demanded of Laura.

'Until she feels well enough to go home,' she'd told him. 'Another week at least.'

'She's a disruptive influence in this house,' Robert had claimed. 'And I think you should be the one to decide whether she's ill or not. As for Neil, he's played nursemaid to her quite enough,' he'd gone on. 'I won't have him forgetting important appointments because of her.'

She'd looked at him then, wondering if she ought to remind him that he, too, had forgotten an important appointment. It had been their twenty-seventh wedding anniversary the day before and although Robert usually booked a table at a quiet restaurant to celebrate the occasion, this time it looked like he had completely forgotten.

Laura had been looking forward to it with more than her usual anticipation, but Robert had spent the day in Edinburgh on business, and had rung to say he and Stella wouldn't be home until late.

'Would it be inconvenient if I brought her home to supper?' he'd asked.

'Of course not,' Laura had told him readily. 'I'll make something nice.'

It wasn't Stella Ross's fault, she'd

reasoned, that Robert had forgotten their anniversary, and she'd welcomed the other woman with warmth and dignity.

The supper had been good enough to grace any celebration, but no-one except Laura had remembered the date and she'd hidden her hurt deep inside.

Her thoughts were interrupted when Robert arrived home just then — bearing a bunch of pale pink, long-stemmed roses wrapped in Cellophane.

She smiled as he bent to kiss her.

'I'm sorry, darling,' he murmured. 'I forgot until I looked at the date on my desk calendar. Happy anniversary. I hope I didn't upset you.'

'Thank you, darling,' she said, accepting the roses and his kiss. 'And you didn't upset me,' she added, trying to forget the hours she'd spent by herself on what should have been a special day.

She had attended a meeting of the Amateur Garden Society, where she had met a new member who'd recently come to live in the area. Laura had found David Croft very knowledgeable about plants, and they'd spent some time discussing their mutual love of gardening. Mr Croft was taking time off from journalism to write a book.

'I decided to leave Edinburgh after my wife died,' he'd explained, 'and make a fresh start here. The house is small and the garden large and pretty overgrown, so I'll have to start from scratch — which will be good therapy when I need a break from writing.'

Laura had listened, fascinated.

'I could help you with the plants and cuttings,' she'd offered.

'That would be wonderful! I'd be glad to have anything you can spare,' he'd told her.

Laura had driven home and there had been warmth in her heart for the rest of the day . . . spoiled a little by Debbie's spat, and Robert's late arrival home, but now he'd brought her pink roses and somehow that seemed to make up for a lot.

'Thank you, darling,' she said again.

Perhaps she was only imagining that they weren't quite so close these days as they'd been at one time. The years, after all, were piling on. Twenty-seven years now since they had married, although she felt as young as a girl when she put her arms round his neck and kissed him.

Robert held her close for a moment, then turned away to examine the mail on his desk.

His dealings on Neil's behalf had to be kept separate from his office, but he frowned when the thought again began to trouble him that Neil was now rather less single-minded about his project than he'd been.

It was Susan, of course. She was distracting him. The sooner the girl returned to London, the better.

Again it was late when Neil and Susan arrived home, and as Laura heard them tiptoe past her bedroom door, she mused that she knew he had several appointments the next day; she just hoped he would be wide awake for them!

Susan's Secret

In the morning, once Robert and Neil had left, Laura took a tray of tea and biscuits up to Susan's room. She swung back the heavy green brocade curtains and turned to smile at Susan.

The girl looked pale and Laura felt sure she hadn't slept very well. She sat down in a chair beside the bed.

'This cup of tea should make you feel better,' she said with a gentle smile. 'And don't rush to get up. You could probably do with a lie-in after your late night.'

There was a short silence then Laura spoke again.

'Susan, I know this is presumptuous of me but — I've asked our family doctor, Dr Grant, to call and examine you. I know you keep telling us that you're perfectly well, but I'll feel happier once he's checked you out. I hope you won't object.'

Susan stared at her with anguished eyes — then burst into tears.

Shocked, Laura looked at the sobbing girl with dismay then took her in her arms, holding her closely with warmth and sympathy.

'Don't you feel well, Susan?' she asked. 'Is that it? Can't you tell me about it?'

She reached for a tissue and the girl mopped at her eyes, fighting to control her tears.

'I . . . I don't need to see a doctor,' she whispered. 'It . . . it's just that I've been unhappy recently about . . . about Rex, my boyfriend. There's been some sort of upset at the place where he works, and I haven't been able to contact him since. I'm so worried.'

Her eyes were like wet violets as she stared at Laura. She had always thought of the older woman as cool and reserved, but now she could see how wrong she had been. Laura's eyes were full of warmth and love.

'Maybe I shouldn't let myself get in

such a state,' Susan said. 'Rex will contact me soon, I'm sure. So please don't bother to send for the doctor,' she implored. 'I'll be OK, I . . . I'm just being silly.'

'Oh, my dear, I don't think you're being at all silly,' Laura said sincerely. 'If a love affair goes wrong, it can be the most painful thing in the world. Sometimes we tend to live our lives through the people closest to us, and if love is shared equally, it can be a wonderful and rewarding experience. But it can also make us deeply unhappy if things go the other way.'

She spoke so feelingly that for a moment Susan forgot her own troubles and wondered about Laura. Had she loved someone and lost him?

Laura rose and walked to gaze out of the window for a moment.

She had spoken from her heart, and again she thought about Robert. She could no longer blind herself to the fact that they weren't as close now as they had been, and she longed to bridge the awful gulf that was growing between them.

She clenched her hands. Susan didn't have to explain anything further, not to her. She knew that her youth and the strength of her love could make her so unhappy that it was affecting her health.

But surely Dr Grant would understand this? He must have dealt with similar problems in the past. Couldn't he perhaps advise the girl on how to relax and try to accept her unhappiness as a challenge which must be defeated?

'I still think it would do no harm to see the doctor,' she said gently as she turned back into the room.

'No, please don't trouble,' Susan protested hurriedly. 'I'll work it out. In fact, I feel better already for . . . for having confided in you. Really I do!'

★ ★ ★

Laura smiled and kissed her cheek, then picked up the tray.

'Would you like breakfast in bed?'

'Oh no, you know me — I don't eat much breakfast,' Susan assured her. 'I'll be downstairs in a few minutes.' She looked at Laura shyly. 'Sorry to be such a nuisance.'

'You're never that, my dear,' Laura told her warmly.

She sighed as she carried the tray back downstairs, her thoughts once again with Robert.

There was no doubt that he was seeing more of Stella Ross these days. They had such a lot in common, and she was a very attractive woman. But what were *her* feelings for Robert? Stella was a very self-contained woman. Was she likely to fall in love with him?

Well, Laura thought, the other woman couldn't love him or desire him more than she did. He was her husband and he meant everything to her.

★　★　★

Susan watched the door closing behind Laura, then she shut her eyes to keep out the pain. They were hot with the tears she had shed — and also with her own inner shame.

How could she have deceived Laura Faulkner like that? Although it *was* true that she didn't need the doctor — at least, not for the moment. But she had the best of reasons for suspecting that all was not well with her — and that she was going to have Rex Windham's child.

It was a secret she had hugged to herself ever since she'd been ill with a virus infection, just after she and Rex had last seen one another.

The very thought that she might be carrying his baby made her feel sick with fear and anxiety, and she wondered anew how she was ever going to get in touch with him. She must see him.

But what had happened to him? She had never stopped wondering that since coming to Fernhurst. Surely it couldn't be true that he was suspected of . . . of what? Of selling some articles belonging to his firm without permission? That was what she'd been told. He might as well have been accused of stealing!

But Rex wouldn't do such a thing! He wasn't like that. Somehow there must be some mistake, she thought, and if only she could see him, and listen to his explanation, things might be a little better.

She thought about the last night she'd seen him. She had gone to visit him at home, after he had been in bed for several days with a virus infection.

She'd taken him some grapes, and several magazines to help him convalesce, and had been surprised and delighted to see that he was making a good recovery. He had seemed very ill indeed just two days before.

It had been a stormy night, and they had drawn the curtains against the wind and the driving rain. The warmth of the fire had been no greater than the warmth of their love, though even then Susan hadn't wanted to commit herself to that love — but Rex had smothered her protests with kisses.

Later she'd insisted on walking home in the rain in order to clear her thoughts. She loved Rex, but her own integrity had also been very precious to her. Now she regretted that she had compromised that integrity and given in to temptation.

She had arrived home soaking wet — and within a week had been laid low with the virus infection which had affected Rex.

As the days passed, she had gradually recovered from the virus, but she had begun to realise with a dawning horror that there could well be another problem ahead for her.

She had shrunk from attending any clinic in order to reassure herself because she was already sure in her own heart that she was pregnant, and had been glad to come to Fernhurst to get away from her mother's anxious eyes.

Now Laura Faulkner wanted her to see Dr Grant, but Susan knew he was the last person she wanted to see! This was something which she and Rex must work out for themselves, and she didn't want to involve the Faulkners in any way.

The sound of voices from the kitchen interrupted her thoughts and she dressed hastily. If she dwelt on her troubles too much, she would be very poor company for the rest of the family. She had tried to get away from it all when she had come here, but it was still with her, and she badly needed to find Rex. Perhaps it had been a mistake to leave London so hastily.

'I was just coming to find you, Susan,' Annie McCall told her when she arrived in the kitchen and wished the others a cheerful good morning. 'There was a phone call for you. A man. But he rang off before I could come and get you.'

'A man?' Susan's heart did a somersault. Was it Rex?

'He said he'd phone back,' Annie's voice went on. 'He was in a call-box and I think his coins must have run out. He just shouted at me to give you the message.'

'Did he give you his name?' Susan asked huskily.

'No, just the message.'

'Thank you, Annie. I . . . expect he'll ring back quite soon, if it's important.'

Susan tried to sound casual as she sat down at the breakfast table. But her heart was beating fast and her hands were trembling.

Rex, she thought. It just had to be Rex. Who else would be interested enough to trace her to Fernhurst? Her colleagues knew she was on holiday but they had no idea where she was staying.

Susan's mind was whirling, but one thing was clear now that Rex knew she was here; she must remain at Fernhurst until he contacted her again. She couldn't risk missing him a second time.

But where was he, and when would he call back?

Her heart was pounding but gradually she regained her lost composure and relaxed and accepted a slice of toast and some coffee.

Annie McCall looked at her shrewdly. There was something up with Susan Ashley, there was no mistaking. She knew it wasn't her place to interfere but she couldn't help feeling sympathy for the girl.

'A nice boiled egg would do you more good,' she told her with mock sternness.

Susan smiled at her; she liked the kindly housekeeper.

'Maybe tomorrow,' she said. 'My appetite's improving every day.'

But in her heart Susan knew she had never felt less like eating in her life.

Rex, she thought desperately, Rex, where are you?

* * *

Debbie had had breakfast earlier with Neil and her father, then she had sneaked a letter which had come in the morning post back up to her room, though she could probably have read it under her father's nose and he wouldn't have asked about it. He cared about nothing except Ross/Faulkner Industries, she thought resentfully, and Neil only caught his attention because he saw Neil's business as an extension of his own.

In the privacy of her room Debbie opened the letter and read it with bated breath. It was confirmation from her tennis coach that a place could be found for her to train in London.

She hugged it to herself and let out a little squeal of delight.

True, she'd have to bear the cost of her living expenses, but there was the prospect of sponsorship to cover the cost of her training.

Her eyes glowed and she felt a great thrill of excitement.

But then, suddenly, she sobered again. Would her great idea work, and how would her parents feel about it? Oh, but surely if they saw how determined she was they wouldn't stand in her way. They just couldn't!

On the other hand, her father might refuse to support her, in the belief that she might choose tennis for a career instead of working for a degree at university.

Debbie's chin firmed. She couldn't let that happen! She had money of her own, but not enough if she was required to pay very much for food and accommodation. Then there would also be travelling expenses each day.

There seemed to be an endless list but Debbie was determined and set about tackling her problem in a business-like way which her father would probably have admired.

She spread out her map of London on the bedroom floor and marked out the area where she'd have to look for rooms. As she surveyed the warren of streets which meant nothing to her, it struck her that Susan would be a good person to consult in this matter.

She managed to way-lay the older girl

as she was finishing her coffee and toast, alone now since Laura and Annie McCall had gone off to change the beds.

'Hi, Susan. Is there any coffee left? I thought I'd have a cup as well,' she suggested. Her air of breathless excitement was apparent, so that for a moment Susan's guilty heart leapt. What had Debbie found out?

'Can I speak to you, Susan?' Debbie asked, her eyes bright.

Susan swallowed nervously and nodded.

Debbie took the chair opposite and leaned eagerly across the table.

'You know that I'm good at tennis?' Debbie began. 'Well, read this letter. I'm supposed to show it to Daddy, but he wouldn't care. He wants me to go to university.'

'That sounds like a fine idea to me,' Susan replied. 'I only wish I'd had that chance.'

'Oh . . . you!' Debbie pouted and leaned back in her chair with exasperation. 'Don't tell me you're like all the rest! I thought at least you would understand.' She regarded Susan with pleading eyes. 'Tennis really is my life, Susan. I love it. I'm really good and I've worked at it, but I need proper training. Do you understand? I'd have loved to have gone to the States, but, of course, it was Neil who got that chance. No-one takes me seriously.' In her desperation Debbie reached for Susan's hand. 'Oh, Susan, please help me. You're my only hope.'

Susan looked into Debbie's anxious face. It was clear just how much all this meant to the girl.

'How could I help you?' she asked simply.

'Read the letter,' Debbie urged cryptically, so Susan quickly scanned the pages.

Once she'd finished she looked up.

'I still don't see — ' she began.

'You could tell me how to get cheap accommodation in London,' Debbie explained. 'I mean, I'd be happy to share an attic or . . . or anywhere . . . anything at all.'

She pulled the city map out of her pocket and spread it out on the table.

'Do you know this area?' she said, pointing. 'Would there be reasonable accommodation around there? I know so little about London, you see.'

Susan pursed her lips. She really did feel for Debbie and thought that she should have her chance. And it would be perfectly feasible for the girl to stay at her own home — but how could she suggest such a thing? Once the Faulkners found out about her condition, they'd hardly think she was a good influence on their young daughter!

She could hardly bring herself to meet Debbie's imploring eyes. She was beginning to grow fond of the younger girl, and to have deep sympathy for her, even as she had sympathy for Mr and Mrs Faulkner.

'I could write to my mother,' she proposed at last. 'Perhaps you could stay with her.'

The girl's eyes lit up.

'Would you? Would you really, Susan?'

'Let me think about it and then we'll see,' Susan said, laughing in spite of her misgivings. The last thing she wanted was to give Debbie false hope.

Debbie threw her arms round her neck and hugged her.

'Thanks, Susan. I've got to rush now,' she said. 'I have training. See you later.'

In a moment Susan was alone once more with her thoughts.

★ ★ ★

When tackling a new enterprise, Robert Faulkner had never been known to let the grass grow under his feet. Neil's new venture had fired his imagination, and although he made certain not to neglect his own business activities, every spare moment was spent working with his son.

Sometimes he felt that Neil's enthusiasm for the memory chips he wished to produce wasn't quite so strong as it had been. As, for example, when they discussed the matter of premises.

'There's a reasonable sized place just become available that might suit you. *And* it belongs to Ross/Faulkner,' Robert informed him as they spent one Saturday morning working in his study.

'It belonged to Telefix,' he went on. 'They made small computers, as you know, but they merged with us a few years ago and now they're planning to expand. They're moving out to new premises south of Melburgh, so their old place will be empty — or may already be empty. I must check on that with Stella — she's been handling their affairs.

'The only thing is . . . Neil!' Robert had suddenly become aware of his son's vague expression as he gazed out of the window.

'Neil,' he repeated. 'Have you heard a word I've said?'

'What?' Neil looked startled — and guilty.

Robert followed the direction of his son's gaze — and caught a glimpse of the tall, slender figure of Susan Ashley in the garden.

She was such a lovely girl, Neil was thinking, with a catch at his heart.

'For goodness sake, Neil, keep your mind on the job, will you?'

Neil cringed at the tone in his father's voice, but he fought to conceal any sign of guilt or embarrassment.

OK, so perhaps his mind *had* wandered, but for the most part he knew exactly how the present plans stood. If he didn't acquire premises at a reasonable rent, then he might as well give up the idea for the time being. His finances wouldn't stretch far just now.

With an effort he recalled his attention.

'I'm listening,' he said mildly.

Robert bit back a hasty retort. It wasn't the first time Neil's attention had wandered when Susan Ashley was around and it angered him considerably, yet he knew he didn't have enough cause to lay down the law. Neil always returned to their discussion ready to pick up the threads and well versed in all the problems.

'I'd have to put Stella in the picture,' Robert commented. 'Though I didn't really want to do that until you were established,' he mused with a frown.

'Why not?' Neil asked. 'I'd have thought she'd be interested.'

'That's just it — she'd be *very* interested,' Robert admitted. 'She'd want to know why we haven't explored the possibilities of memory chips on behalf of Ross/Faulkner.'

He gazed out of the window for a moment.

'You know, Stella's a very hard-headed businesswoman, though sometimes . . .' He paused, then went on, 'Sometimes she confuses me,' he admitted.

Neil regarded his father with interest as the older man turned back to look at him.

'She's not nearly so predictable as I would have believed.'

He sighed deeply, then a determination came into his eyes.

'However, I'm going to risk telling her, and I'll ask her to rent the Telefix premises to you. My guess is that she'll be delighted to get the building off her hands.'

* * *

As it happened, however, Stella Ross wasn't at all delighted. Robert chose to walk into her office and ask for five minutes of her time just when she was studying the figures for Telefix after their first year as part of the Ross/ Faulkner empire. The figures were disappointing to say the least, especially since heavy expansion was planned.

Stella frowned, knowing that she'd been a prime mover in absorbing that company. Robert had advocated caution, but she'd refused to listen and had exercised her own judgment — wrongly, it seemed now.

So when he mentioned the vacant building, she stared at him for a moment.

'What's on your mind, Robert?' she asked.

'That's what I like about you, Stella, you go straight to the point. As I always say — '

'There's no sense in wasting time,' she interrupted.

He looked slightly ruffled, she had decided, like a normally-calm pool of water which had been disturbed by a capricious breeze.

'Well?' she asked, looking at him expectantly and leaning her arms on her desk.

'I know someone who needs the Telefix buildings,' he told her.

'So do I,' she retorted. 'I'm seriously considering preparing a report for our next meeting which would reverse some of our decisions over Telefix.'

Robert regarded her with surprise.

'I think we should leave them in their old premises,' she continued. 'That new complex would bring in something really worthwhile on the open market, so why should we put Telefix there?' There was a gleam in her eye as her voice rose a little. 'Honestly, Robert, their expansion just isn't justified.'

'Give them time, Stella,' he advised, cautious of any rash moves. 'Say three years, not months.'

Stella regarded him in horror.

'Oh no, it's been a great deal longer than that!'

'Well, it isn't three years,' Robert insisted. 'Surely we can stand poor returns from them for a few more months? It was your hunch, Stella, so give yourself a chance,' he pleaded, afraid that Stella's decisions might ruin his plans for Neil.

Quickly he changed the subject. 'Now, what about the building that Telefix is to vacate?'

'Which firm wants it?' Stella asked.

'Neil's.'

Her eyebrows raised sceptically and he hastened to explain.

'He's just starting up, sure, but he has all the know-how at his fingertips for the manufacture of memory chips,' he told her, trying to sound confident.

Her eyes sharpened and she sat tapping her ballpoint pen between her fingers.

'Why must he be independent?' she asked.

'It wouldn't employ many people,' Robert explained, 'and it'll require all his brains and expertise to set it up. He wants to do it for himself, and I agree with him.'

'Then what's the problem?'

'Finance. He can't exactly go splashing it about.'

'None of us can,' Stella retorted crisply. 'It'll do him good to have a few setbacks. It'll toughen him up,' she remarked. Then: 'Tell him no, Robert, he can't have it.'

He looked at her steadily. She was completely unpredictable. He had expected her to want to help Neil for . . . well, for his sake. He had thought she was beginning to like him a little, perhaps even a lot.

'It has to succeed, Stella,' he insisted, 'and we have to help him.' He hesitated slightly then went on, 'You see, I've put

Fernhurst up as collateral against a substantial loan from the bank.'

'You've done what?' she asked, staring.

He grimaced. 'I know — but that's how sure I am that the boy is on to something good. He'll make a go of it. I know he will,' he insisted, but she detected the note of strain in his voice.

'What does Laura think about your putting up Fernhurst?' she asked.

'She doesn't know,' he told her flatly.

Suddenly he reached across the desk and covered her hand with his own.

'And she mustn't know . . . ever,' he insisted. 'You're the only one who knows, apart from Neil.'

'You must be mad,' she said, yet the tone of her voice was a great deal less strident than before. She couldn't help feeling a warm glow in her heart. So Robert had taken her into his confidence, even before his wife!

She allowed his hand to grasp hers, then she put her other hand on top of his.

'Oh, Robert, you fool!' she said softly.

'I'd better not be,' he said, and as their eyes met in a long gaze, they knew they understood one another. 'I told you because I knew you'd understand,' he said. 'It's a risk, I admit, but I have to do it.

'So, can I have those premises?' he finished.

'I'll think about it,' she hedged, and looked away from him, but his grasp tightened, compelling her to meet his earnest gaze.

'Oh, all right,' she conceded, 'Neil can have the place — but the rent must be reasonable,' she cautioned.

'Reasonable,' he agreed, adding. 'but not his last ha'penny.'

She met his look and nodded, then they both sat back in their chairs, satisfied with the done deal. Satisfied, too, with the way they worked together, and stimulated by the friendship which was building up between them.

'If Neil turns out anything like his father, he'll be a very lucky man,' Stella said softly.

Face To Face With Rex

The following evening at Fernhurst the telephone rang just as Susan was about to go to her room to get ready for the evening meal.

Mrs McCall answered it and called after her, 'It's the gentleman! The one who phoned before.'

Susan's heart leapt with hope, and she raced along to the telephone in the hall. Her fingers trembled as she lifted the receiver.

'Hello? This is Susan. Who is it?' she asked anxiously.

'It's me — Rex.'

'Rex!' She almost cried with relief. 'Are you back at the flat? Rex, I have to see you . . . ' Her words seemed to run nervously on until he interrupted.

'Susan, darling, take it easy,' he said. 'It's OK. You'll see me within the next half-hour, if that's all right. I'll come to

'. . . Fernhurst? Is that the name of the place?'

'No!' cried Susan almost wildly. How could she talk to him if he came here? The Faulkners would all want to see him and talk to him, and she had to see him alone. But . . . but where was he?

'You don't mean you're here in Melburgh?' she asked.

'I certainly am,' he told her brightly. 'I've checked in at a guest house near the post office. It's called Lochinvar.'

'Oh, yes, I know it,' Susan acknowledged breathlessly. 'Just stay there please, Rex, and I'll come to see you straight away.

Rex hardly had time to say goodbye before she hung up.

Susan didn't know which way to turn. Her legs had turned to jelly. She could hardly believe she was going to see Rex at last.

She turned towards the stairs, feeling as if she were living in a dream. But just then the front door opened and Laura Faulkner walked into the hall with a tall, middle-aged man following behind.

Her eyes brightened when she saw Susan.

'Ah, there you are, Susan,' she called. 'Come and meet Dr Grant. He's a very old friend of our family, and I'm sure it'd be better if only you'd let him check you over.'

Susan's eyes had opened wide with shock at the mention of the doctor's name, and she hardly listened to Laura's low, sweet voice after that. All she could feel was panic bubbling inside.

She just couldn't let Dr Grant examine her — especially with Rex waiting for her.

'I . . . I'm so sorry,' she gasped, 'I . . . I've no time just now. I've got to go and meet a friend . . . '

And with that she bolted out of the front door without even stopping to pick up a jacket.

She almost ran all the way into Melburgh so that she was breathless by the time she reached the Lochinvar guest house.

Rex had been watching for her, and he met her at the door. After a quick hug, he led her into the lounge, which was otherwise empty.

'Goodness, did you run all the way? You're out of breath!' he exclaimed.

He kissed her and held her close for a moment.

'It's great to see you again.'

'Rex, we've got to talk,' she said, drawing back at last. 'Where have you been? Is it true that you've been suspended from your job?' She looked at him with imploring eyes. 'That's what they told me when I enquired after you at Mortimer's. But it can't be true! Oh, Rex, why didn't you get in touch with me?'

'Calm down, love,' he said, taking her hand to guide her towards a comfortable-looking settee drawn up in front of the fireplace. 'One question at a time. I did try to phone your home, but no-one answered, and then I heard you were in bed with that virus infection. Of course I wanted to see you, darling, but I thought I'd better wait until you were better. I didn't think your mother would want me to visit — especially since it was probably me you got the infection from!'

Susan vaguely remembered the phone ringing one day when she was ill in bed and her mother had been out. She'd tried to reach it but her legs had been like jelly and she'd never made it. The next thing she'd known, she was waking from fitful slumbers and the telephone ringing had seemed like a dream.

She noticed Rex wasn't looking quite as confident as he usually did. With darker colouring than Neil Faulkner, and not quite so tall or well built, it seemed strange to see him in such unfamiliar surroundings. Yet he didn't look as worried as she would have expected in the circumstances and this puzzled her. Did that mean it was all some ghastly mistake? Surely that must be the only explanation.

'What happened, Rex?' she asked

earnestly. 'Have you resolved the mix-up now?'

'It wasn't a mix-up, Susan,' he said quietly.

She stared at him, shocked.

'You mean . . . you did sell some of the stock without putting it through the books?'

He waggled his head and ran a hand through his hair.

'Well, it's a long story — and it involves someone else.'

'Did you?' she repeated, determined to know the truth.

'Yes, I did,' Rex admitted, 'but as I say, that isn't the whole story.'

'And you're still suspended, and the investigation's still going on?'

He nodded, and she could see now that he looked very worried, though he shrugged quickly and smiled.

'Forget it, darling. Forget everything except that it's weeks since I've seen you. Come here . . . '

He tried to draw her back into his arms, but she pulled away. She felt so terribly confused and uncertain, but the fact that Rex was still in trouble and there had been no mistake about the missing stock only made things seem worse. Even if someone else was involved, he shouldn't have allowed it to happen. And one thing puzzled her — nobody at Mortimer's had mentioned anyone else being involved . . .

'I said we've got to talk,' she insisted, 'and I'd better tell you straight. I think I . . . I'm having a baby. That night . . . Oh, Rex . . . I've been so worried.' She couldn't keep the tears from welling over.

He stared at her and she could see that her news had shaken him.

'You're sure?' he asked, his expression grave.

'As sure as I can be. Mrs Faulkner — the lady I'm staying with — wants me to see the doctor, but she just thinks I'm run down. As a matter of fact, that's why I ran here — I shot out of the house to avoid seeing this doctor friend of hers, Dr Grant.' She looked at him anxiously. 'I wanted to keep it to myself for the meantime.'

'Well, it's no problem,' Rex said, though his eyes were bleak. 'We'll get married, of course. I won't let you down, Susan.'

She swallowed, looking at him unhappily. Did she still love him as much as she had done? She felt so confused that she hardly knew how she felt.

Besides, how could they marry with this investigation hanging over his head? What sort of start would that be for a future together?

'I'm not sure that we love each other enough, Rex,' she said quietly, gazing down at her hands. 'I . . . don't know what my feelings are any more. And besides, I think we ought to resolve a few things first of all. Like this trouble you're in. Can't you at least tell me how it came about?'

He hesitated. He had never discussed the affairs of Mortimer Antiques with her, and he wondered how much he ought to tell her now. It wasn't entirely his affair and he wasn't sure that she would understand in her present mood.

'No, I can't, not yet,' he said bleakly. He gazed at her, his thoughts in a whirl. She must need him very badly at the moment and he felt torn in two. But he was certain of one thing — he loved her very much.

'I love you, Susan,' he told her simply, 'but maybe you have to consider the future more deeply. So long as you know that I'll stand by you whatever you choose to do. We both bear the same responsibility.' He leaned forward and kissed her. 'You're not on your own in this, my love.'

She sighed a little. Rex's kisses hadn't stirred her as they might have done at one time.

Her feelings seemed to be frozen; she no longer knew how she felt about anyone.

'I must go,' she said, standing up.

'I'll see you back to Fernhurst,' he offered.

'No, please don't do that.' She looked at him anxiously. 'I don't want the Faulkners to know just yet — that there's anything wrong, I mean.' She stopped, not trusting herself to go on. 'How long are you staying here?' she asked instead.

'I'll stay as long as you need me, or . . . or until I have to go back to London.'

'I see. Well, I'll get in touch with you tomorrow,' she said.

* * *

Out in the fresh air, she turned her steps towards Fernhurst, and her thoughts switched to Laura Faulkner and Dr Grant — and the way she had run out on them. What must they have thought of her?

She glanced at the time. The doctor would be holding his evening surgery now. On impulse she turned up one of the side streets which led there. Perhaps Mrs Faulkner wouldn't be so upset by her appalling behaviour if she went and apologised to Dr Grant.

It was nearing the end of surgery and there were few patients left. She didn't have long to wait before she was shown into his surgery.

He was writing up some notes, but as he looked up to welcome his next patient his eyes widened with surprise when he recognised Susan.

'I've come to apologise,' she told him quietly. 'I don't know what you must think of me for running out like that.'

His eyes twinkled kindly in understanding.

'You're not the first patient to run out on the doctor,' he assured her.

'I haven't seen Mrs Faulkner yet, but I feel awful,' she went on. 'She's been so good to me.'

His keen eyes swept over her, noting the pale complexion and the anxiety in her eyes.

'Oh, I'm sure there's no harm done. Laura's a very understanding woman,' he said, then went on casually, 'But now that you're here, why don't you let me give you that check-up? The nurse could help you to prepare.'

'No.' She stared at him, biting her lip. 'I . . . I think I know what it is. I . . . ' She gulped, then rushed on: 'I think I may be pregnant. I hope I can tell you that in confidence,' she added anxiously. 'I don't want to tell anyone else until I decide what I want to do.'

'I see.' He nodded understandingly. 'You're not married?'

She shook her head.

'But Rex — my boyfriend — that's who I was dashing out to see this evening — anyway, he's said we'll get married but — well, marriage is a big step. I'd have to think about that more deeply.'

He looked thoughtfully at her.

'Don't you think we ought to make sure about a possible pregnancy before we get ahead of ourselves here?' he asked. 'And as to the matter being confidential, I can reassure you of that.'

She smiled at him, grateful for his

calm understanding, and let him begin the tests that would confirm or deny her pregnancy.

As she left the surgery, Susan felt an overwhelming sense of relief to have shared her burden, though naturally she was still anxious about the results of the pregnancy test.

★　★　★

When she saw Dr Grant again he greeted her with a smile. 'Well, my dear,' he began, 'I can assure you that you're not pregnant.'

She had unconsciously been sitting on the edge of her seat but now she slumped against its upright back, an overwhelming sense of relief flooding through her.

'I think your virus infection pulled down your general health and your own anxiety aggravated this,' the doctor continued smoothly. 'A good vitamin tonic will work wonders and I'd be very surprised if you're not in tip-top condition very shortly.'

She hardly heard the rest of his words. The sudden release from the strain of the last few weeks was proving too much for her and her eyes filled with tears as she thanked him for his kindness.

'You needn't worry any more,' he told her gently. 'It's best to remember, though, that you should always make sure about your health rather than worrying yourself sick over nothing.'

'I'll remember. Thank you, Dr Grant.'

Susan wiped away her tears, but although her relief was great, it couldn't take away her sense of guilt. There would be no baby — but there might have been. What would the Faulkners say if they knew? And Neil? She didn't want to think about that.

Neil's Proposal For Susan

Laura Faulkner planned her day so that she could spend an hour or two in the garden. She felt at odds with herself and the removal of weeds from the borders was often quite therapeutic.

She had been upset with Susan after the very embarrassing way she had run out of the house the other evening when Laura had wanted to introduce her to Dr Grant. But this morning, the girl had been to the surgery and had returned looking much more composed.

'I'm so sorry about that, Aunt Laura, and I've apologised to Dr Grant, too,' she had said. 'I was just feeling a bit overwrought. But Dr Grant has recommended a tonic and he says that'll soon put me right.'

Susan was now talking about returning to London, though Laura had persuaded her to stay on at Fernhurst for a few more days. In a funny way she seemed to be a good influence on the family. Debbie hadn't been so sulky recently, thanks to Susan, and Neil, too, wasn't working flat out as he used to do.

Laura sighed deeply as she tried to remove the long tendrils of a piece of ground elder. Robert was the only one who hadn't made any effort to entertain their guest, and he was the only one, too, who . . .

'Oh, dear, that sounds as though you've got a whole heap of troubles.'

The man's voice made her jump. She looked up to find David Croft from the gardening club looking down at her with a rueful smile.

'Have I called at a bad time?' he asked. 'Mrs McCall said to tell you she's just put the kettle on.'

She smiled. 'I'd better come in then! It's nice to see you, and you couldn't have called at a better time — I could do with a bit of company at the moment.'

'It's a beautiful day, isn't it? Let's sit out here on the bench,' he suggested.

Laura pulled off her gardening gloves and dropped them into a basket beside the bench.

'How's your garden progressing?' she asked. 'I promised to give you a few plants, didn't I?'

'It's coming along. It isn't quite the wilderness it was,' he informed her with satisfaction. 'I've cleared a corner ready for alpines. Actually that's why I've come — I was hoping to beg a few specimens.'

'I'll do my best for you,' she promised.

He was looking round very appreciatively.

'You love gardening, don't you?' he observed. 'You can always tell the difference between genuine love and a mere tidy-up to keep the neighbours from talking.'

She laughed. 'Yes, I do love it,' she agreed, gazing around her with no small satisfaction. 'Robert — my husband

— loves flowers but hates all the hard work. We've someone to help with the heavy work, of course, but you know there's so much more to gardening than that.'

He regarded her appreciatively. It was nice to hear her laugh; he could sense that Laura Faulkner wasn't a woman who had much opportunity for laughter. Her face was too grave, her eyes too serious.

'That sigh I overheard made it sound as though you had the weight of the world on your shoulders,' he commented. 'Is there anything wrong?'

'No, nothing,' she protested quickly, then flushed. Sometimes it was good to talk to a stranger. 'Well — just small family things,' she admitted. 'My son, Neil, is starting up a new business — in computers — and I'm not at all sure that it's the right thing for him. I feel he's a technician, not a business manager — but his father obviously thinks otherwise.'

'Perhaps he can do both,' David

suggested diplomatically.

She nodded slowly. 'Perhaps. Robert's encouraging him. I don't know how far their plans have progressed but — well, it's silly really, but there's just something . . . a small niggle somewhere which makes me anxious. But perhaps I'm worrying about nothing,' Laura continued, shrugging her shoulders.

'We can't help being the kind of people we are,' David Croft told her gently. 'Worrying about people a little shows that you're a caring person. I wish I had someone to worry about me!'

Their conversation was interrupted by the arrival of Mrs McCall with the tea. David rose to help her.

'And do you need worrying about?' Laura asked him with a teasing smile as she poured out the tea.

'Oh no, not really. I manage very well. But it would be nice to have a woman about the house to check to see if I've gone wrong anywhere when I'm entertaining and such like. Speaking of which, would you and Mr Faulkner like to come to supper on Friday evening?' he asked eagerly.

'Robert's already made other plans,' Laura said regretfully. 'The Chamber of Commerce.'

Stella Ross would be going with him. It was happening more and more frequently, Laura had noticed, and he never enquired if she minded or if she ever got lonely when she was left to her own devices.

She glanced sideways at David Croft. He was a nice-looking man, she mused: sunburned, with greying hair that was still plentiful, and if not exactly handsome, his looks were clean-cut and appealing. She liked his keen eyes, and the fact that he understood so quickly anything she tried to explain. Robert never had time to listen . . .

'I could come myself,' she suggested hesitantly.

He looked pleased. 'That would be grand. Will seven o'clock be all right? We'll have time to look round the garden before we sit down to eat.'

'That'll be lovely, Mr Croft.'

'Please — call me David.'

'David.' Laura smiled. 'And, of course, I'm Laura.'

She felt suddenly happy and excited. How nice to have something to look forward to.

★ ★ ★

Susan had persuaded Debbie to talk to her parents about the chance she had been offered to join the tennis training programme in London, and once Susan had assured them of her certainty that her mother would be happy to accommodate the girl, they had been given the go-ahead to pursue the idea.

So now Susan had written home with the request and they were waiting for the response.

Although Susan hoped to return home herself shortly, Laura had asked her to stay on for a few more days, a suggestion to which she had agreed since she wasn't particularly looking forward to the slightly dull grind of her secretarial work.

She had also been to see Rex again, of course, to break the news about her non-pregnancy. His relief had been every bit as great as her own.

'I'm so glad for you, darling,' he'd said. 'I know how worried you were. But it makes no difference to us. We'll still get married.'

She'd stiffened a little.

'I . . . I don't think so, Rex,' she'd said dully.

'Oh, but — please think about it, Susan. I do have a problem to solve, I admit, and it does concern a . . . a lady. But it's a bit complicated to explain to you.'

'No need to explain anything, Rex,' Susan had said, pushing his arms away from her.

So, it involved another woman! For a moment she'd felt strangely hurt.

'I love you, Susan,' Rex had insisted, 'and I want to marry you, just as soon as . . . as this issue of my career is resolved.'

'I hope your lady friend will also be happy when it's resolved,' she'd said tartly.

'She doesn't know there's been this trouble,' Rex had told her quickly, too wrapped up in his problems to be aware of what Susan thought or felt about the lady he'd mentioned. 'That's why I want to keep it to myself for now.' He'd eyed her anxiously. 'I will explain it all to you as soon as I can, I promise.'

She'd shrugged. 'It's none of my business,' she had replied a little sharply. 'Anyway I've promised Aunt Laura I'll stay for a few more days, then I'll have to go back home.'

'I must go tomorrow,' Rex had announced, 'to make myself available for the investigation, but I'll get in touch again, I promise.'

He had pulled her to him and kissed her, but again Susan's response had been lukewarm and he'd soon let her go.

She didn't know how she felt about Rex, but she was worried over what he had become embroiled in, and the fact that it involved another woman had shaken her.

* * *

On the evening after Rex left for London, Neil came home early and persuaded Susan to accompany him to the theatre in Edinburgh. He'd been given two tickets and wanted to make use of them.

'Dinner first, then the theatre,' he suggested happily. 'We might as well make the most of the fact that I'm free earlier than usual. It's because I can't do anything now until I hear from London about some equipment. There's been a hold-up somewhere,' he explained, 'and there's no point in waiting around.

'I've set up an office in Melburgh for the moment, but I hope to move to the Telefix building within the next two weeks, and then — ' He stopped abruptly as he realised he was talking business.

'Sorry,' he apologised, looking rueful. 'I didn't mean to bore you. Maybe the theatre will make up for that:'

'I'm not bored,' she said quickly. 'Not at all.'

And it was true. Now that she was feeling so much better, she was getting back some of her old vitality and hearing about his business concerns piqued her interest.

He left her then to make a quick visit on business, and she sat on in the garden, musing that she would be sorry to leave Fernhurst. It was a lovely old house with gorgeous grounds. But she missed her own family, and besides, she was beginning to feel the need to be busy again. It was just a shame her own job was so mundane.

She went indoors to check the time. She would have a leisurely bath then change into a nice dress. Perhaps she'd even tie her hair up. Suddenly she found herself looking forward to the evening with an enthusiasm she hadn't felt for a long time.

The telephone rang as she started up the stairs, and when she picked it up, a bright, competent voice asked for Mr Neil Faulkner.

'This is Duffield Components,' she was told. 'There's no reply from Mr Faulkner's Melburgh number. I wondered if he happened to be there? He gave us this as his home number.'

'This is his home number,' Susan said swiftly, 'but I'm afraid he's out at the moment. Would you like him to call you back when he comes in, or perhaps I can give him a message?'

'Will you please hold the line?'

Susan waited, using the time to find a message pad and ballpoint pen. Shortly afterwards a man came to the telephone and asked her if she would take the message.

It was quite complicated and Susan had to repeat it carefully to be sure that she had noted the details correctly, but she was well used to dealing with such calls at her office and had no difficulty in setting it out clearly and concisely.

Neil returned shortly after she'd hung up. She relayed the message, and gave him the notes she'd made.

'They were closing down for the weekend,' she explained. 'If the message isn't clear, you can ring this number on Monday morning at nine-thirty, and speak to Mr Finch.'

For a moment he looked dismayed that he'd missed the phone call, but then he scanned the notes and his face broke into a smile.

'This is terrific!' he exclaimed. 'The detail of these notes mean I can work over the weekend with a few of my men, assembling the new equipment. And it's thanks to you. It's lucky you were here!'

He looked up at her, his eyes alight. 'We'd better enjoy our evening, Susan, for by the looks of things it'll be my only time off for ages!'

* * *

It was a lovely evening and Neil's eyes often strayed to Susan's pure profile instead of the stage. The play was a comedy and her ready laughter was very infectious.

Going home, Neil stopped the car at a spot overlooking the night-lit cityscape. She looked unbelievably beautiful in the pale blue, rather ghostly glow of the moonlight.

'You're the loveliest girl I've ever seen,' he told her huskily. 'I thought you were beautiful when you first came, but now that you're feeling better, you look wonderful.'

'Thank you,' she said, smiling shyly. 'And thank you for a lovely evening. It'll be something to remember when I go back home, though I've promised your mother I'll stay on here for a few more days.

'Debbie wants to go to London, you know, and my parents have offered to have her stay with us — if your parents agree. But your mother wants to think it over a little longer.' She hesitated a little. 'I rather think she wants to discuss it with your father.'

This was said rather diffidently. She wasn't very sure of Robert Faulkner. She had won all their hearts except for his. He viewed her with reserve. Although he had conceded to Neil that she was a lovely girl he seemed to resent any time he spent with her.

'It's a fantastic opportunity for Debbie,' Neil said. 'But I'll miss you. Debbie, too, of course,' he added hastily. 'I'll miss you very much indeed.'

For a moment he gazed longingly at her, then he leaned over and took her into his arms, kissing her gently at first then with increasing passion.

She yielded at first — but then she was pushing him away as she remembered Rex. A sense of guilt assailed her and she knew she wasn't ready to establish any warmer relationship with Neil than she had already.

'I — I'm sorry,' he said rather thickly.

'I didn't mean to offend you.'

'I'm sorry, too,' she whispered, 'but . . . I don't want things to change between us, Neil. I like you very much, but I don't want anything more from . . . from anyone at the moment.'

'Has someone hurt you?' he asked quietly.

'No, not really. Look, I can't talk about it. I hope you'll understand.'

Her cheeks grew warm as guilt swept through her again. What would he think if he could see into her heart?

'I think we'd better go home,' he said, and she could sense his disappointment.

At Fernhurst Susan said goodnight and would have gone upstairs, but Neil caught her arm.

'Don't go yet, please,' he said. 'Come into the sitting-room. I want to talk to you about something else. Please, it's only for a moment.'

Susan couldn't ignore his plea. 'All right,' she conceded.

She followed him into the sitting-room and perched on the edge of a chair. He sat down opposite her.

'Do you have to go back to London just yet?' he asked bluntly.

'Why? What's on your mind, Neil?'

'Well, I need a secretary, and I wondered if you'd consider taking the job. I think we could work very well together. You don't have to decide right now, but think about it over the next day or two, will you?'

'I don't think that would be a very good idea!'

They both spun round, startled, as Robert Faulkner walked into the room.

'Neil, I want a word with you,' he said sternly.

Susan's cheeks paled. What had he found out?

Neil rose to his feet as his father walked into the sitting-room, his heart sinking as he noticed the signs of anger in his face. What had got his goat this time?

Neil acknowledged that his father was a great help to him, but he wished the older man would let him stand on his own two feet sometimes and make his own decisions.

Suddenly pale, Susan would have hurried from the room if Neil hadn't caught her arm. She looked at him anxiously but there was a steely determination in his eyes as he turned to face his father.

'I'm perfectly capable of choosing my own secretary, Dad,' he said quietly. 'And I've already asked Susan. But if there's some reason you think she shouldn't accept the job, then I think she ought to hear it, too.'

He felt Susan's body tremble slightly and he pressed her arm reassuringly.

'Very well, she will hear it, too,' Robert said dryly. 'I called in at my office to pick up some papers on the way home today, and I found this note on my desk, typed for me by my secretary.'

He produced a typewritten sheet and held it out to Neil.

'Duffield Components,' he said crisply. 'They couldn't reach you in your new office. They had an urgent message for you and had to get our home number from my secretary.' He looked coldly at his son. 'And why couldn't they reach you, Neil? I'll tell you why — because most of the time you're too busy entertaining Susan, that's why.'

His voice was tight with anger as he glared at Neil, then turned to look at Susan.

'Oh, maybe I shouldn't blame you, my dear, but before you came Neil was in complete command of his affairs — and on a project like this, believe me, he needs to keep his whole mind on the job. Instead he's neglecting his work in order to spend time with you.'

He turned back to Neil and brushed a hand anxiously through his hair.

'I'm sorry, but there's just too much at stake. You know we're out on a limb on this one, Neil,' he implored. 'I insist that Susan returns to London immediately, and you put your back into getting this project off the ground.'

Neil was staring at him, his mouth tight with anger.

'If you'll let me get a word in, I might explain something to you,' he said sharply. 'Duffield had told me there was a hold-up, and there seemed little point in sitting in the office for the rest of the afternoon without being able to accomplish anything useful.' He noticed his father was about to object but held up a hand to silence him. 'No, listen, Dad. I knew they could reach me through you, if necessary, and that's precisely what happened. They telephoned here.'

He picked up his briefcase and produced the notes Susan had taken.

'Look over these, will you?' he asked, thrusting them at Robert. 'Susan took the call and I think you'll agree that no one could have made a better job.'

Robert took the notes and began to read over them, aware of Neil's determined glare boring in to him. His son's vehemence had taken him by surprise.

131

Susan turned pleading eyes on Neil.

'If you'll excuse me I'll just say goodnight,' she said in a low voice.

Neil touched her arm briefly.

'The offer still stands,' he murmured. 'We can talk it over tomorrow.'

Once Susan had gone Neil turned to his father.

'Well?' he asked tersely.

'Yes . . . I agree this is cèrtainly a competent job,' Robert admitted. 'But I still stand by some of my remarks, Neil. You do need to be single-minded over this, and a girl can take up a lot of your time.'

'She could also be a great help to me, as you should know.'

Robert looked at his son thoughtfully. Perhaps he was right. But there was so much at stake!

'Very well, Neil,' he conceded, 'if that's what you want, I hope she accepts your offer. But, as I say, we need every ounce of dedicated effort to launch this project of yours.'

★ ★ ★

After Neil, too, had gone upstairs Robert sat on for a while, alone with his troubled thoughts. He was worried about the way things were going, but he couldn't discuss all of those worries with his son.

As yet the lease hadn't been prepared for Neil to rent the Telefix building, and Stella Ross didn't appear to be in any hurry.

At first he'd merely thought it was an oversight, but when he'd phoned Stella to quiz her about it, she'd laughed softly.

'We can talk about that outside business hours, Robert,' she'd said. 'Why don't you drop by for a bite of supper, then we can see what can be done?'

'All right, but I'll have to work here until eight o'clock at least.'

'Eight-thirty will be fine,' she had assured him lightly.

He had gone straight there from the

office without going home to change.

When he'd rung the doorbell of her flat, she had come to the door wearing a soft silk kaftan in delightful shades of nasturtium and peach. It made her look very feminine and even more attractive than usual.

'I've made something special tonight,' she said as she took his coat in the hall.

Robert was a little taken back. He hadn't expected any elaborate preparations.

'I'm afraid I can't match you for elegance, Stella.' He laughed a little awkwardly. 'I'm still in my working clothes.'

'Have a wash, if you want to,' Stella offered. 'Or even a shower. There's plenty of hot water.'

Leaving his jacket outside, he was removing his collar and tie in the bathroom when Stella tapped lightly on the door.

'There's a cardigan here, Robert, which belonged to my father. Maybe it would be more comfortable for you.

I'll leave it on this chair outside the door.'

'OK, thanks, Stella,' he called back as the bathroom began to fill with steam.

He felt refreshed after a quick shower, and dressed quickly.

He opened the door — and saw the cardigan Stella had put there for him. In soft grey cashmere, it would certainly be more comfortable than his formal suit jacket. With only the slightest hesitation, he lifted it and slipped it on.

He looked and felt greatly refreshed when he joined Stella. She gave him a quick kiss on the cheek.

'You're a very elegant man, Robert Faulkner,' she said lightly. 'Now let's have supper.'

It was a delightful meal, and once again Stella was an equally delightful companion. She constantly amazed him with the way she could step into two different rôles: the hard-headed businesswoman and the beautiful hostess.

He relaxed and enjoyed the evening, hardly noticing the time passing as they finished their meal, then sat together on the sofa in front of the fire. He was hardly aware of doing it, but it seemed the most natural thing in the world to take her hand and hold it as they talked. Presently Stella leaned her head on his shoulder, then reached up to kiss him — and he found himself kissing her in return.

The clock chiming ten broke the moment. Robert started and drew back, and he suddenly remembered the reason for his visit.

He smiled teasingly. 'You've got me lulled into such a relaxed mood, I almost forgot what I came for! It was to ask you about the Telefix lease. I thought you were attending to it right away?'

'Oh, Robert, darling!' Stella smiled. 'Surely we can talk about that at the office? Please, let's just relax for now.' She gazed at him fondly. 'We need an evening like this, you and I. We can't work at high pressure all the time, and you're the only man I know who could surely understand.'

She sat up straight and squeezed his hand. 'Let's have more coffee,' she suggested.

'Not for me, Stella. I must be going,' he protested. For him the spell had been broken.

He saw a sudden glint in her eyes. Stella had wanted him to leave in her time, he thought shrewdly, not in his.

But already his mind had switched to his work.

'I really have to go over the Rutherford papers at home,' he explained — and remembered that the very file he wanted to work on was still on his desk. He glanced at his watch.

'Darn it — I'll have to go back for it,' he said.

'Forget the Rutherford file!' Stella declared, laughing, but Robert could sense her underlying annoyance.

'That's all very well for you to say,' he returned lightly, 'but I'm the one who's dealing with it.'

'You'd have more time to deal with at work if you didn't help Neil so much,' she commented, her tone suggesting she was teasing, but Robert could still sense those dangerous undercurrents.

That had all happened earlier this evening, and now he sighed as he lifted the Rutherford file out of his briefcase.

It had been when he had gone back to the office to pick it up that he had found the message from Duffield for Neil, and it had angered him — although perhaps it wasn't so much anger as irritation. Irritation at Neil, and at himself for failing to have got an answer from Stella.

In spite of his worries, he soon become absorbed in the work, and it was a couple of hours before he surfaced, stretching in the chair and flexing his shoulders. It was with some surprise that he noticed it was after one o'clock.

As he put the file away, he pondered

yet again on Stella Ross. She was making no secret of the fact that she enjoyed his company and was attracted to him. She'd even said that spending an hour or two with her couldn't possibly hurt Laura in any way — but now he was beginning to wonder quite what she had in mind.

Was the price of the Telefix lease an even closer relationship with her?

Laura had gone to bed, which was unusual for her. She was beginning to lead her own life these days, Robert mused as he climbed the stairs — and he wasn't sure that he liked it. But then, he had only himself to blame. He was so obsessed with his work.

Suddenly he felt older and very much alone in the quietness of the house — the house that was at risk if he didn't get the Telefix building. And Stella knew it.

Doubts And Fears

Susan had also spent a largely sleepless night. She was due to return to London with Debbie on Saturday, and to take up the threads of her life once more, and she had wakened up wondering why she didn't just stick to that plan, say goodbye to the Faulkners, and put everything behind her.

Her parents were happy to have Debbie to stay with them, and now that no obstacles stood in the girl's way, Susan had helped her with all the arrangements, once Laura and Robert Faulkner had finally agreed that she should have her chance.

'She'd never forgive us if we stopped her,' Laura had told Robert when she had persuaded him to put his papers aside for once so that they could talk about it over breakfast. 'I mean, even if she doesn't become a top-class player, she'll know she's tried. And as for her studies — well, there are openings for her to pursue them later. But it wouldn't work the other way round, would it, Robert?'

She had put her slender hand on his. It was a lovely hand, small but well shaped, and slightly roughened by her work in the garden.

Robert had looked up at her, suddenly realising how well she looked. She looked fresh and — sparkling. Was that the result of her companionship with this new garden club friend, David Croft?

'You've had your hair cut,' he'd noted. 'It's nice — it suits you.'

Laura's eyes had flickered. She'd had it cut several days ago, and he'd only just noticed! Was his mind so full of Stella Ross that he hadn't even time to look at her these days?

However, she'd learned over the years that the best way to fight for Robert was to do it with great patience and with her very own weapons. Stella wouldn't have him, she had vowed to herself in the quiet of the night. He was hers and she would never give him up.

She'd smiled sweetly at him.

'The new style was Susan's idea. She thought it would suit me better.'

It did flatter her, as did the pretty scarf at her throat. Her skin was softer than Stella's, he'd noticed, and her grey eyes as clear and innocent as pools of water on a bright summer's day.

'We'll have to let her go, Robert,' she'd said, returning to the subject of their daughter. 'My goodness, we let Neil have enough chances when it comes to business matters. It's only fair that Debbie should have the same opportunities. It's time we took more of an interest in her tennis.'

'Oh, very well,' Robert had said grudgingly at last, 'she can go — but if she doesn't make a success of it, then in future she takes our advice.'

★　★　★

It had been arranged for Susan and Debbie to travel back to London together, but now Neil had offered Susan that job — and something in her was responding to the offer. She *wanted* to stay at Fernhurst and work with Neil.

And yet if she did, wouldn't she, in time, feel obliged to tell him about her affair with Rex and just why she had been so afraid when she'd first come to Fernhurst?

She was beginning to have great respect for Neil, though she denied in her heart that any deeper feeling was involved. But something in her was sorely tempted to be with him, and to work with him every day.

It would certainly be exciting, much more exciting than returning to her mundane job in London.

Neil came to find her shortly after breakfast the following morning.

'Well?' he asked without preamble. 'Have you thought about my offer? What's it to be? And please don't worry about Dad because he won't object.'

His eyes were bright with hope as he waited for her decision.

Susan looked at him, wondering what she ought to say. She felt he was asking her to make a big decision, one that could alter her whole life.

'Well . . . well, OK,' she agreed at length, 'I'd like the job. Thank you, Neil,' she said firmly.

His eyes glowed as he bent forward and kissed her lightly.

'That's to seal the bargain.'

'OK — but there are one or two things to be ironed out first,' she warned. 'I still have to go back to London with Debbie. I want to settle her into my home and show her the ropes for travel and all that sort of thing. And there's my present job to consider, too. I'll have to give notice and so on.' She eyed him anxiously. 'Can you afford to wait a week or so?'

'No problem,' he agreed briskly, 'though I'd like you to be as quick as you can. I'll keep the paperwork going myself, and leave some things for you to catch up on — but I do need you.'

'I can see that,' she conceded. 'I'll be back as soon as I can, if . . . if Aunt Laura doesn't mind.'

'She's delighted at the prospect,' Neil assured her. 'She enjoys having you in the house.'

Susan smiled. Now that her main worry had been lifted from her shoulders, she had enjoyed the hours she had spent lately with Laura.

The older woman had asked her opinion on her wardrobe and together they had sorted through Laura's clothes. Susan's natural sense of style had been brought to bear so that Laura now had a much better idea of what suited her in terms of colour and style, and they had been shopping together, too, to update her whole look. Laura was delighted with her makeover, and Susan had loved doing it.

'I like your mother,' she told Neil simply. 'We get along very well.'

★ ★ ★

On Saturday, Laura, Robert and Neil Faulkner were all at the station to wave goodbye to the girls.

Debbie's eyes shone with excitement.

'I'll work hard, Daddy, I promise,' she said fervently. 'I'll make you proud of me.'

'We're proud of you now, darling,' Laura said rather huskily as she hugged her, and Robert nodded. Now that his mind had been made up to this venture, he would help Debbie in every way possible.

'You'd better be good,' he growled, slipping an envelope into her hand. They grinned at one another and Susan noticed just how alike they were.

Neil kissed his sister, then deliberately kissed Susan as well.

'Come back soon,' he whispered.

It was very quiet at Fernhurst after Susan and Debbie had left for London, and Laura found the hours passing slowly.

With the help of Annie McCall, she spring-cleaned the house to keep herself occupied as a spell of wet weather prevented her from working in the garden. She was missing Debbie and Susan more than she would have believed.

She was thankful that Susan was returning to Fernhurst, otherwise she might have worried about Neil. He and Robert had been closeted in the study for hours on the evening after the two girls had left for London and Neil was again beginning to look tense and sober-eyed.

He mustn't turn himself into another business machine like his father, she thought, as she stitched on fresh clean cushion covers. Neil was more like her. He needed to take time for the beauties of this world, as she did with her flowers and plants.

She was glad that Susan seemed to recognise that Neil needed that sort of relaxation and slowed him down.

Robert, on the other hand, she mused, revelled in the buzz of making a successful transaction, competently accomplished in record time.

Laura glanced at the time and decided that she must freshen up for dinner. David Croft was coming this evening, and Robert had promised to be early for once.

The previous week she'd spent a delightful evening at David Croft's cottage, which she had found he was renovating with skill and taste. She had eaten an excellent curry he had made himself — no carryouts for this bachelor! — then they had spent some time out in his garden, which was also being redesigned, much to Laura's delight.

'I thought I'd try to create a rockery here,' he told her, as they contemplated an awkward corner.

'Mmm . . . yes,' she conceded thoughtfully, 'or you could put a few flagstones there, and I'm sure I could find you a few interesting containers. Trailing lobelia, perhaps, petunias, geraniums . . . that sort of thing would be lovely and give you some extra colour.'

'It's a thought,' he agreed, 'though I've a few good stones here to put in a rockery.'

'Of course you need a rockery, but what about that other corner?' she suggested.

Together they argued amicably over this corner and that, then David suggested coffee and they returned to his spacious sitting-room.

'This is nice,' Laura said, looking around appreciatively. 'If I lived on my own, this is exactly the kind of house I'd choose.'

'I thought you wouldn't be able to contemplate anywhere but Fernhurst,' he said, looking at her searchingly.

Was she happy with Robert Faulkner, he wondered. He was a fine man, a man of stature in the community as he'd discovered from remarks made by local people, but he couldn't help wondering . . .

Ah well, he thought, sighing, that was Laura Faulkner's private life and nothing to do with him.

Nevertheless, he viewed her as a very beautiful woman and extremely pleasant company.

David's eyes sobered as he thought about his own late wife, Melanie. He still missed her so very much, and although he'd done his best with the cottage, he knew there were several small touches still to be made which would give that indefinable touch so natural to most women.

Should that ornament be on the fireplace, or would it look better on a table? And what about the curtains? Were they right for the room?

He voiced his doubts to Laura, and in no time at all, she had moved things around so that the room looked freshly charming and inviting.

'What a difference,' he said, delighted.

She went on to suggest swapping round one or two small pieces of furniture, which they did together.

'But what a way to entertain a dinner guest!' he added ruefully.

'Oh, not at all! I'm having a lovely

time,' she assured him happily, her cheeks warm with exertion, and her eyes sparkling with laughter.

'Now — your curtains.' She eyed them consideringly. 'Colourwise they're fine, but they're a bit on the long side. But if you've got a work-box anywhere, I could lightly stitch up a hem for now.'

He was enjoying her friendship so much, he thought happily, as they drank coffee together later, chatting about the latest books and art exhibitions which were on in London.

It would be so easy to demand more of her time than she could spare, he thought.

A faint warning note sounding at the back of his mind — it would be so easy to allow this woman to become important in his life.

Consequently he was a little reserved and more circumspect when she invited him back to Fernhurst for dinner on the following week.

'My daughter's going to London with

Susan,' she explained. 'She's actually going to do a great deal of training for top-class tennis,' she added proudly. 'We'll miss her though, and I'm afraid I'll find I've rather a lot of time on my hands.

'So, David, if there's anything more I can do, just say the word,' she added sincerely. 'But in the meantime do come along and have dinner with Robert and me. We could do with being cheered up!' she pressed him.

He looked into her shining eyes. She was a lovely woman, he thought. She had an indefinable quality of charm which made him feel better for knowing her.

He was very lonely without Melanie and he wanted to warm his heart in the friendship of an attractive woman. But couldn't it . . . wouldn't it cause him heartache in the future if he let himself be attracted in this way? She would be hard to resist.

David Croft put the thought behind him and accepted the invitation.

Now Laura looked round with satisfaction. She and Annie had made a good job of the house, and the old place shone with polish. She'd picked flowers and arranged them carefully in vases and bowls throughout the house, on cabinets and small tables, and their scent perfumed the air.

Fernhurst had never looked more elegant.

Laura chose a soft, swirling dress in whisper-pink which brought colour to her face. She used make-up very sparingly, but Susan had taught her that a tiny touch of colour could bring her face to life quite charmingly.

As she checked her appearance in the bedroom mirror, she was pleased and excited at the difference which Susan's advice had made to her appearance. She looked younger than she had done for years.

Robert was late in arriving home, but Laura was expert now in planning a dinner which could wait for a few more minutes if need be. David had arrived on time, and together he and Laura had been tempted out to walk round the garden.

Laura had shown him her new little pool of sparkling water which she hoped would be a great feature of her garden.

'Water lilies,' she explained, 'that's what I hope to have. Would it be awful of me to try to find a little mermaid?'

They laughed together.

'It would be delightful,' he said, but his eyes lingered on her bright eager face and the charming picture she made with the truly beautiful garden as her background.

By the time Robert came home they were deep in conversation, and as he stood in the doorway, he suddenly saw Laura as David Croft must surely see her. He felt a sense of shock. Sometimes he'd felt that Laura was inclined to make herself colourless, but now he could see how wrong he was.

She was as delicately beautiful as his finest piece of porcelain.

He thought about Stella Ross's spectacular beauty when she dressed up in the evening. No, Laura's beauty was not at all spectacular, but now he saw that it was all the more arresting for that.

Stella had left a message with Neil that she wanted to see his father that evening, but for once Robert had made a note in his diary that he was particularly required to dine at home. He wanted to meet David Croft and get to know him a little better. He wanted to see the man who was beginning to take up so much of Laura's attention.

'I've already told Mum I can't make dinner this evening,' Neil told his father as he cleared his desk. 'I want a word with Andy Fellows — you know, the architect — about the Telefix building. I know it doesn't need much in the way of conversion, thank goodness, but some alterations have to be made, and I hope we can make a start soon. I've got my workforce all ready now. Is it all going ahead as planned, Dad?'

'Oh . . . certainly,' Robert said, as confidently as he possibly could.

In fact, Stella was holding it out under his nose like a carrot before a donkey, he thought angrily. But for once she was going to be disappointed. No way could he run to do her bidding this evening.

'I must get off home,' he told Neil. 'I don't want to keep your mother waiting. She was making a special effort this evening.'

Robert was more silent than usual as they all sat down to dinner, but he was very much aware of Laura as she and David Croft had a meeting of minds which sometimes eluded him. She talked knowledgeably about something of which he knew nothing, yet she'd often been shy and retiring in the presence of his business friends.

Was this how she felt when he and Stella Ross discussed business? Did she feel left out?

He watched her, noting how deftly she attended to their guest, and how effortlessly.

'You have a beautiful home,' David Croft commented admiringly.

'Yes, we love it, don't we, darling?' she said to Robert.

How silent he was, Laura thought. He'd answered the comment with one or two brief words, and she looked at him from under her lashes as she poured the coffee.

How much did Robert really love Fernhurst? It had always been her home, but not his, though he now owned it.

Sometimes she almost felt as if he'd bought her with the house — and as if they both came second in his life after his business.

Doubts constantly plagued her. Did he still love her? How much did he really care?

It was late when David Croft went home, too late for much conversation as Laura and Robert went upstairs together.

Surely he must love her, she thought, though even in their closest moments, she couldn't ask him.

Robert didn't sleep for a long time, but lay awake thinking about all that was most precious to him: this woman who was his wife, this house which was his home, and the fact that he was in danger of losing them both.

Laura would surely hate him if he lost Fernhurst through the sort of speculation she always distrusted.

It was too terrible to contemplate, he thought, in an agony of mind foreign to him. He'd always been so full of confidence in himself. Now that too was ebbing away.

Susan Meets 'The Other Woman'

Susan agreed to work a week's notice and to show her successor the ropes before she took up her new job. She had also taken Debbie around and showed her how to use the Underground and the buses, so that she'd be able to get about reasonably easily.

All in all, Debbie was settling in very well, and Helen Ashley, who was a great tennis fan, had taken to her at once. They had spent a long time together discussing the finer points of the game.

'It'll never take the place of football for me,' James Ashley told them.

'He's always bored when Wimbledon comes round,' Helen said ruefully. 'I need support, Debbie. I'm glad you're here, my dear.'

On the Tuesday night Susan arrived home from her office and learned that Rex had been to see her. In fact, her mind had been very much on Rex for the past day or two, though once again she had failed to locate him. She very much wanted to get to the bottom of whatever trouble he was in. But although she passed the large show-rooms and auction rooms of Mortimer Antiques on her way to the office every day, there had never been any sign of Rex.

'He couldn't wait until you arrived home, dear,' her mother said. 'I explained to him that you're working late some nights to clear your desk before you leave. I think it came as a shock to him to learn that you've decided to move to a new job in Scotland.'

'I wanted to break the news to him myself, and I *have* been trying to get in touch with him,' Susan admitted. 'But — he isn't the easiest person to find these days.'

Mrs Ashley was still uneasy about Susan. Now that her health was so much improved she wished she could be more like Debbie. Debbie was so dedicated to her career and so competent that surely her future was all mapped out for her.

In contrast Susan never seemed to know exactly what she wanted from life. Was it Rex Windham? Helen wasn't sure if Susan still loved him or not. Indeed, she had wondered if the girl might not be attracted to Neil Faulkner, but their relationship appeared to be purely business.

If only she could see their only daughter settled in life, how happy she and James would be.

'Rex wants you to meet him at some restaurant on Friday evening,' she told Susan now. 'He seemed anxious that I might forget so he wrote down the name on an old envelope for you. Here — '

'*The Montpelier, Friday 7.30,*' Susan read.

'He said you'd know where it is,' her mother added.

Susan nodded. They'd gone to The Montpelier a few times in the past. It was a quiet place so she knew that Rex must want to talk to her.

Thoughtfully she turned the envelope over in her hands. It was addressed to Rex — and she saw now that the sender's name and address had been written across the top of the back of the envelope. Rex had opened it carelessly, but if she closed it again carefully, she could make out the name and address —

'Miss Stephanie Mansfield,' she murmured. 'It looks like . . . sixteen Greenbank . . . Court.'

The rest was too frayed to be read easily.

Stephanie Mansfield! She looked at the stylish handwriting and recalled Rex saying that the trouble he was in involved someone else. A woman!

She stared at the name. How did it concern a woman? And was it *this* woman?

Something about the name and address caught her imagination and she had an instinctive feeling that she was on the right track.

Susan was no longer sure what her feelings were for Rex, but it certainly wasn't the hot, searing passion she'd once felt for him. However, there was enough feeling left for her to be very concerned for him, concerned for his welfare.

She had to know what sort of trouble he was in, and to see if there was any way she could help him.

She finished her supper quickly, then put on her coat and picked up her bag.

'I've got to run an errand, Mum,' she explained. 'I'll be back as soon as I can.'

She was going to try to find out what had happened at Mortimer's.

She had borrowed Debbie's map of London and traced Greenbank Court. It was pretty out of the way, and she had to take two buses.

When she finally walked down the avenue of tall terraced houses, which had mainly been turned into flats, she felt increasingly nervous. Supposing Rex also happened to be visiting this Stephanie Mansfield! How embarrassing that would be!

Her steps faltered as she neared number sixteen, then her chin firmed and she walked quickly up the steps and rang the bell.

It seemed an eternity before a young man came to the door and stared out at her.

'Miss Mansfield?' she asked anxiously. 'Miss Stephanie Mansfield?'

'Door across the hall,' he informed her cheerfully. 'This is sixteen A. She lives in sixteen B.'

'Oh, I see,' she replied, and crossed the hall to ring at the door indicated.

After a few moments the door opened and a woman looked out.

'Stephanie Mansfield?' Susan asked again, in a small voice.

'Yes, what can I do for you?' the woman asked.

Susan stared at her, speechless. She

had never been more astonished in her life, for the woman who was looking curiously at her was far from the beautiful girl she had envisaged. Instead she found herself staring down at a very small old lady with grey, wavy hair and a small, pleasant face.

A pair of very dark blue eyes regarded Susan with interest and humour, somehow amused by her evident bamboozlement.

'Can I help you?' she asked.

'Er . . . ' Susan was at a loss for words, but she struggled to pull herself together. 'My name is Susan Ashley. I — I'm a friend of Rex Windham's.'

Immediately Miss Mansfield's face lit up and she threw the door of her flat open wide.

'Do come in,' she invited. 'I don't have many visitors these days, so you're most welcome, Miss Ashley — and if you're a friend of Mr Windham's, then you're even more welcome.'

She led Susan through a small hallway to the living-room.

'Please — have a seat here by the fireside,' she said. 'I'll just put on the kettle — I'm sure you'd like a cup of tea.'

Susan sat down obediently on the Queen Anne-type chair with the rather faded green velvet cover.

While Miss Mansfield was out of the room, she took the chance to look around her. It was a fairly large room, but sparsely furnished with well-polished inlaid mahogany and rosewood furniture. One or two paintings with heavy gold frames hung on the walls, and there were several unfaded sections of wallpaper which suggested that other paintings had been removed.

The room was very clean and well kept, but there were few ornaments, except for one or two old photographs in silver frames and an ornamental plate on the mantelpiece.

Susan's eyes were drawn to one particular photograph of a lovely young woman dressed in the style of the mid-Twenties. She stood up to have a closer look at it.

The woman was sitting with a large Labrador dog at her feet. Behind her were the beautiful terraced gardens and fine façade of an elegant Georgian house.

'That's Thornpark, my old home,' said a voice behind her, as Miss Mansfield entered the room with a tea tray in her hands.

Susan started rather guiltily.

'I'm sorry,' she said. 'I didn't mean to be nosy — I was just admiring your photographs.'

'Myself as a young woman,' Miss Mansfield informed her. 'I was living at home with my parents then. I never married, you know. Not many young men came back to my part of the world after the war.

'Now, my dear, do you prefer lemon or cream?' she asked as she set the tray down.

'Cream, please — no sugar,' Susan replied, and accepted a cup of tea out of the most delicate china cup she had ever held in her hands. It had a design of pale pink roses with a fluted rim decorated in gold.

'I saved some of my china,' Miss Mansfield was saying happily. 'There are some little luxuries I can still afford, thanks to Mr Windham. Do have a biscuit, my dear.'

Susan hesitated then accepted the thin wafer biscuit.

Miss Mansfield presided over her tea table with grace and dignity. She wore a rather shapeless blue silk dress, but her shoes were very neat and of excellent quality.

'I miss Thornpark, of course,' she went on. 'I expect Mr Windham might have told you, but I kept it on as long as I could after my parents died, for the sake of Armstrong and his wife. They lived in, you see, so it was their home, too. But when poor dear Ted died and Edith went to live with her sister, I knew I had to let it go.

'Unfortunately, though, the debts had been mounting up since my father's time and there was a mortgage to pay off.' She sighed deeply.

'The solicitor found me this flat and I brought what I could here out of Thornpark. Then it was sold. But, gradually, I've had to sell my pretty things — as Mr Windham will no doubt have told you.'

Susan bit her lip.

'I — I'm afraid Rex doesn't know I'm here, Miss Mansfield,' she confessed. 'I only came because . . . well, because I was rather worried about him having been suspended from work.'

Miss Mansfield's smile faded.

'Suspended? What do you mean? Is he in some sort of trouble?'

Susan's thoughts began to whirl. So this sweet old lady knew nothing about what had happened to Rex!

Then what *had* happened to him? What could he have done, and how did it affect this woman?

'Mr Windham has been so very kind,' Miss Mansfield went on. 'I approached Mortimer's, you know, about selling some of my good ornaments and pictures, but I confess I was disappointed with the valuation they offered. I thought it was rather low.

'It was an older man who first came with young Mr Windham, and he was supposed to be the expert, but later Mr Windham came back with a great deal more money for me. He appreciated the true value of my antiques, you see,' she told Susan fervently.

'I had so many debts after moving from Thornpark I didn't know what to do and the extra money was a godsend. But thanks to Mr Windham, I'm much more comfortable now than I have been since life became so difficult at Thornpark.

'He's a wonderful young man, and so competent. Surely his firm must realise that?' she asked, gazing anxiously at Susan.

'Yes, of course,' Susan said quickly. She didn't yet know what Rex had done, but he had certainly earned the admiration and respect of Miss

Stephanie Mansfield.

Presently Susan rose to go, and Miss Mansfield smiled sweetly at her.

'Please do come and see me again, Miss Ashley,' she invited. 'Ask Mr Windham to bring you. He does come to see me from time to time, you know.'

They shook hands at the door, and Susan hurried home with her thoughts in a whirl.

There was nothing in Miss Mansfield's flat to indicate that Rex had done anything wrong. Instead he'd helped the elderly lady, and the antiques which Mortimer's had bought from her must surely be genuine.

She would ask Rex as soon as she saw him, and get to the bottom of this once and for all.

* * *

The next morning Debbie received a letter from her parents while Susan got a note from Neil.

She couldn't deny the small flutter of

excitement in her heart when she recognised his bold, firm handwriting, and she slipped the envelope into her jacket pocket. She would read it later, when she was alone. She knew that she was hoping it would be at least affectionate.

Debbie, on the other hand, opened hers at once.

It was from her mother, with a few lines added by her father. She could no longer complain that her parents weren't taking an interest in her.

'Annie McCall's dog has had puppies,' she announced excitedly. 'Oh, I hope Mum keeps one for me! I'll write and ask her. Oh, and Elizabeth Grant — that's Dr Grant's daughter — has got engaged. Good for her!'

Dr Grant! The muscles of Susan's stomach contracted even as her fingers tightened about Neil's letter. She wanted to return to Scotland very much, but always the spectre of Dr Grant and their shared secret seemed to hang over her.

It was no use. She would have to write to tell Neil before she went back to Fernhurst. She couldn't live under such a shadow, and she couldn't keep any secrets from him. After that, it would be up to him whether he wanted her to return or not.

Slowly she opened his letter and again her heart fluttered as she read the boldly-penned words which left her in no doubt that he missed her very much.

He also expressed his anxiety about the lease of the building where he was soon to begin production.

'I can't understand the hold-up,' he wrote, 'but if it lasts much longer, all our plans and our hard work — Dad's and mine — are in danger of coming to nothing. I can't keep everything in limbo for much longer.

'I'm longing for you to come back, and I'm going to need you very badly, especially when we have this delay . . . '

She read on and on. He was paying her the compliment of confiding in her and Susan put the letter away, her

173

thoughts full of Fernhurst.

She must confide in Neil. It was the only way.

* * *

Robert Faulkner was also thinking about his son the following evening as he locked up his office. He was due to have a talk with Neil at home, but first he knew he must pay yet another call on Stella Ross.

He'd checked and he knew that she had left the office early — and that she'd left a message to say that if he wanted to contact her, he could do so at her home.

Robert felt he was being torn two ways as he turned the car in the direction of Stella's home instead of Fernhurst. It was happening more and more these days.

Something in him was repelled by Stella, by her undoubted self-interest and by the hard core in her which made her even better at business than he was himself. Always a small seed of doubt prevented him from being entirely ruthless in his business affairs, but she had no such inhibitions.

Most of the recent Ross/Faulkner successes were due to her dealings. And although she had made mistakes in the early days, she was now making up for them by cutting out the dead wood — rationalising the workforce, she called it — and reshaping the whole company.

She had no need for the Telefix building, Robert knew, but she was holding it over him as a way of ensuring that he would call on her in the evenings, ostensibly to discuss the matter but, in fact, to give her an hour or two of his company.

Robert was under no illusions as to what Stella had in mind, and as he parked his car then rang the doorbell, he couldn't help his senses quickening.

This time Stella had left her flamboyant clothes in the wardrobe and was wearing a soft, simple, demure top in palest pink cashmere. Even her make-up was sparing and she looked delightfully feminine as she welcomed Robert warmly.

'You're not in a hurry, Robert darling, are you?' she asked, smiling with affection, her dark eyes very alluring.

She hadn't been at all pleased when Robert had insisted on going home early the evening Laura had invited David Croft to dinner. Stella had taken very special pains that evening over her own cooking. She had wanted Robert to call in casually, and had planned to serve him something so delicious that he was sure to be impressed by her wide ranging talents ... and perhaps stay a little longer. But her plan had been ruined when he had gone home to his wife's bidding.

Eating supper by herself had been a frustrating experience, and she had laid the Telefix lease aside once again. If Robert wanted it, then he could have it. But on her terms.

'I can't stay long,' he said briskly now, although he was already beginning to feel dangerously attracted by her perfume and by the whole intimate set-up. Stella had the gift of making him relax. It was so tempting to lounge in one of her very comfortable armchairs by the fire, and have a drink before eating something she had cooked.

She always managed to produce something unusual, and even now as she pushed open the door into the kitchen, he could smell the aroma of delicious food.

'I'm just cooking a bite of supper for myself,' she called brightly. 'There's enough for two, if you like. It's so light it won't even spoil your appetite for dinner later.'

'Thanks, but I'd better not stay,' Robert insisted, as she sailed back into the room with two glasses of wine on a tray.

'Have this then, Robert. It's a new wine I haven't tried before. I'd be interested to hear what you think.'

She sank down on the arm of his chair, kicked off her pretty pink sandals and stretched out her dainty feet.

'Isn't it gorgeous to wind down after working together all day? It often amazes me how well we get on, you and I.' She fingered the rim of her wine glass and gazed thoughtfully at him from beneath her dark lashes. 'I've been meaning to tell you that,' she began, 'and to say thank you for your patience with me when I first started. After all, I made some awful mistakes. Thank you, darling,' she said softly, then smiled as she leaned forward and kissed him.

Impulsively his arms went round her, holding her close.

She was an exciting woman. Her perfume was faint but very sweet, and her whole personality seemed to be much softer than usual.

Sometimes, in their business relationship, he tended to forget that she was a woman, but tonight he was forgetting that she was his business partner!

Her arms crept round his neck, and

once again she kissed him with growing passion.

'Oh, Robert,' she whispered, 'we're so right together. Can't you stay, darling? Stay with me for a while,' she pleaded.

Robert felt they were right together, too — so right that it frightened him.

A warning bell seemed to sound in his head, and with an effort he wrenched himself away.

'No, I can't,' he said hoarsely. 'It wouldn't be fair.' He looked at her, his eyes soft and pleading. 'Stella, you know I didn't come to see you. I came — well, I came for the lease. It's just that you keep sidetracking me.'

He looked down at the rich carpet and felt terribly confused. He couldn't deny that he found Stella extremely attractive, but he had to keep his initial aim in mind for he knew he had too much to lose.

'I've got to have it,' he continued, fixing his gaze upon her. 'Or I'll lose everything — including Fernhurst. Please, Stella, sign the lease.'

She glared at him and he could see the glitter of the firelight in her dark eyes, but there was also something else there. Shocked, Robert realised there were tears.

'If I let the lease go,' she began, her voice tight with emotion, 'then I let you go, and I want you, Robert,' she said simply. 'I want you very much.'

Robert swallowed. He'd never seen Stella like this before. She was always so in control.

She looked up at him. There were still tears in her eyes, but this time her voice was hard and cold, almost businesslike.

'You want the lease, Robert, and I want you,' she stated. 'There — that's my price.'

He was stunned. Her words gripped his heart with fear.

'But I'm married!' he reminded her hoarsely. 'I'm not free, Stella. Have you forgotten that?'

'As if I could! But please try to understand, Robert.' Her voice was shaky with emotion. 'This is very hard for me — but it's something I have to do.' She looked at him longingly. 'If you felt the same way . . . ' Her voice tailed off.

When she spoke again her expression was bleak, her eyes full of anguish.

'You can have the lease in two days — if you agree to my terms.'

Robert stared at her with horror.

'You can't mean this!' He grasped her shoulders. 'Look,' he said, 'let's discuss this sensibly . . . '

But Stella shook him off.

'I do mean it, Robert!' she said, and he felt threatened by the steely determination in her voice. 'Don't make this any harder for me. Let me know your answer in two days.'

He stared at her for a few moments more then, without a word, he walked out the door.

Robert had never been in such torment. To his shame, part of him wanted to pay Stella's 'price' for the Telefix lease, gladly and willingly. She had been so honest about her feelings for him that he couldn't help being flattered, and he couldn't deny that he found Stella Ross exciting.

If he went to her in two days' time, he would have his lease and the price to pay would bring excitement and pleasure, if not happiness, to them both. And no-one need ever know.

But *he* would know, and he would be taking everything that he and Laura had together away from her. He would be cheating his wife.

And wouldn't he also be cheating himself? Surely he had more pride and dignity than to stoop so low?

Yet if he didn't go to Stella, he might cheat Laura just as drastically for he would be in danger of losing Fernhurst, the place she loved so much.

No, he must go to Stella.

Robert rubbed his face with his hand, feeling that his brain was in turmoil. If he did go to Stella, he would despise himself for his own weakness, and for allowing her to get the better of him.

How could he be attracted to a woman who was willing to resort to blackmail in her desire for him? And what if Laura found out? If her lovely clear eyes began to look on him with reproach . . .

* * *

'Is there anything wrong, Robert?' At dinner the following evening, those same clear eyes looked at him with concern. He seemed to be living entirely within himself these days, thought Laura, and his appetite had become very poor. In fact he had offended Annie McCall who had cooked dinner for them the previous evening by suggesting that she might be a bit more adventurous in the kitchen!

'I know many a body would be glad of it,' he told Laura, 'but it's boring nevertheless.' He had added a few even more pointed remarks and had eaten hardly anything.

Annie had said nothing, but afterwards Laura had found her crying softly into the warm, furry flank of one of Flossie's puppies.

'Please don't upset yourself, Annie,' Laura had said soothingly. 'Mr Faulkner's just tired. Unfortunately it tends to make a man's stomach sour!'

'It's good plain food, Mrs Faulkner,' Annie had told her. 'I've been at Fernhurst all my life, even in your father's day, and no-one has ever objected to good plain food.'

'And lucky we are to get it,' Laura had insisted. 'Tell you what, Annie. I'll do the cooking tomorrow night. I'll try to think of something he might enjoy — and if he turns his nose up at it — well, this time he'll have me to deal with!'

'We've never had this sort of trouble before . . . ' Annie had begun darkly.

Before what? Laura had wondered. Before Stella Ross had come into his life? But her mind had shied away from answering that question.

In an effort to pique his appetite she had taken great care this evening preparing an Italian dish which they had enjoyed while on holiday in Rome two years before. However, in spite of the appetising aroma rising from his plate and the glass of specially chosen wine at his elbow, he was still toying with his food, and he looked startled when Laura asked him if there was anything wrong.

'Of course not,' he said with a quick stab of fear in his heart. Did she know anything? Did she know about Fernhurst?

But of course she didn't. It was only his own nerves, his own guilty conscience, which were at fault. But he dared not discuss anything with her in case he let a careless word slip.

'What could be wrong?' he countered.

'I just wondered if — if you were enjoying your meal. It's that Italian dish you liked so much in Rome. I made it specially.'

Rome! That was in the days before Neil had finished his training and was planning to study in America. Gilbert

Ross had been alive then, and Robert had been full of confidence in his own ability to look after both Ross/Faulkner Industries *and* his own private life with equal efficiency. But now it seemed to him that he could do neither!

What appetite he had had vanished and he pushed the plate away.

'Sorry, Laura, but you'll have to excuse me,' he said. 'I've got to get on with some work in my study for an hour or so. Thank you for the meal.'

His manner was so brusquely polite that she felt rebuffed.

There was something seriously wrong with him, she decided. She couldn't remember a time when he had been off his food like this.

The only one to be considerably cheered up was Annie McCall, who was glad to see that Laura's Continental food had fared no better than her own plainer offerings!

★　★　★

Laura walked round to David Croft's cottage the next morning with no excuse other than that she wanted a willing ear to listen to her troubles.

'Have you come to see how my rockery's getting on?' he asked.

'Rockery?' she echoed blankly, then, 'Oh . . . rockery!' she repeated. 'Oh yes, of course.'

He laughed. 'Forgive me, but obviously you haven't! In that case, you must have come to drink my excellent coffee and let me treat you to a chocolate biscuit. Let's spoil ourselves, shall we?'

While they were drinking coffee, he watched her keenly, hoping to see a lightening of the shadows on her face.

What a beautiful face it was, he thought. It was the sort of face which grew more beautiful the more he saw of it. She had a broad, intelligent forehead framed by her new hairstyle, and her clear grey eyes had an innocence which told him that she would never be more to him than a good friend.

Her love and loyalties were all for Robert Faulkner, but those qualities only served to make David admire her even more.

She was the only woman who would ever have a place in his heart besides Melanie, he told himself, and he would be proud to love her even if she could only give him the warmth of her friendship in return.

'Do you want to tell me about it?' he asked gently.

Tears welled in her eyes and suddenly she was sobbing and fumbling for her handkerchief. He put his arms round her and stroked her hair reassuringly.

'That's it — you have a good cry, then we'll try to see if we can't make it better.'

'It won't come better, David,' she said huskily. 'I don't think Robert really loves me. I know that I should never even think such a thing, never mind say it — but I think I came with the house.'

He looked at her with concern.

'Oh no, Laura, I'm sure you're wrong . . .'

But she wouldn't let him finish.

'No, no, I'm not,' she insisted. 'Robert bought it, you see, from my father. It's always been my home — but only his since we married. But I . . . I've always loved him. And now I'm afraid he . . . he's found someone else.'

Laura faltered over her words and fresh tears filled her eyes.

'I don't believe it!' David Croft said stoutly. 'I think that's your imagination, Laura. I've seen you two together, and I think Robert Faulkner cares very deeply for you.'

'I wish I could believe you,' she sighed. 'But there's something wrong, and it's something to do with me. I can feel it. I know him, and I know when it's just a business deal and when it's something more personal. And this time it's — something personal.'

She couldn't explain further. She certainly couldn't tell him that Robert had no expression of love whatever for her now, even in their private moments. What more did she need to show her that something was drastically wrong?

But David did appear to understand because she could feel the sympathetic tightening of his arm about her shoulders.

'If you're really worried, can't you talk to him again? Can't you get him to talk to you?' he suggested.

She bit her lip, considering.

'I suppose you're right. He won't be home until late this evening, but tomorrow Neil's going to Edinburgh and I'll have Robert to myself . . . I hope!' She nodded, making the decision. 'I'll make him talk to me then.' Her grip on the arm of the chair tightened unconsciously as she declared, 'I've got to know where I stand with him. I've just got to.'

She looked up at David.

'You're right, David, this problem isn't going to go away until we've talked it out.'

As she sighed wearily and leaned back in her chair, he had to resist the temptation to take her in his arms. All he wanted was to comfort her, care for her, love her.

Instead he smiled reassuringly and kissed her cheek.

'Just remember that you are a very lovely woman, Laura Faulkner. Remember that when you talk things out with him.'

Rex Confides

Neil Faulkner worked late most nights to keep his paperwork up to date, and knew he'd be glad in every way to have Susan back again. He'd rung her in London, but he'd only got Debbie, who was full of excitement over her new life in London, and who informed him that Susan had gone out to supper with Rex Windham.

'That's her boyfriend,' she'd added.

Neil's chin had firmed. He was used to fighting for what he wanted, and he wasn't giving up, either on his business or on Susan.

In fact, Susan had spent some time that evening writing a very difficult letter to Neil, a letter which made her heart quake with fear now and again. Suppose he refused to understand how she had felt about Rex? Suppose he didn't believe how much she regretted what had happened between them, something for which she had paid so dearly in pain and anguish? She had valued her own integrity so highly that she now felt she had let herself down most of all.

But now that Neil had confided his deepest worries to her, she was returning the compliment and telling him about her own worries and fears. She couldn't live in apprehension each day in case he somehow found out the true reason why she had gone to see Dr Grant.

He had to know, even if it meant he would no longer want her to come back to Scotland.

Shutting her mind to that thought, she posted her letter on the way to see Rex.

The other great worry in her life was this trouble which surrounded Rex. Unlike Neil, he hadn't confided in her fully. She knew he had been virtually accused of stealing, but what, exactly, had he done?

Rex was waiting for her when she arrived at the restaurant that evening.

'Do you want anything before we have supper?' he asked. 'I've managed to get us that quiet table in the corner.'

How often they had sat at that very table and talked about every subject under the sun. They had always been good companions, even when she had known that her love for him was greater than his for her.

But something had happened to her at the culmination of that love, she thought. It had burned itself out, her passion for him quenched by the fear and anxiety that she was pregnant, which was something Rex was unable to understand.

For a long time she had felt nothing, and the reason for that had partly been her anxiety for him. Now at last she felt she was beginning to live again.

He was still looking at her enquiringly, and she remembered his query. She shook her head.

'Let's just go to our table and order.'

The waiter hovered attentively as they scanned the menu.

'I fancy the paella,' Rex mused. 'How about you?'

'Yes, fine, I'll have that, too,' Susan said. She didn't feel she could eat much in any case, so it didn't really matter what she ordered.

She waited until the waiter had taken their order, then leaned forward, eyeing Rex directly.

'You might as well know,' she told him, 'that I've been to see Miss Mansfield. Her address was on that envelope you left with my mother.'

Rex stared at her in dismay.

'Oh, good gracious,' he said. 'You — you didn't say anything to her, did you? I mean, about me?'

'I told her you've been suspended from your job, but I couldn't tell her why, because I don't really know, Rex, do I? You've never explained it to me properly.'

He sat back with relief.

'Well, that — that's OK then. Only I

don't want her to find out, Susan. It would really worry her, you know?'

'Find out what?' she asked.

'Well . . . ' He ruffled his hair. 'I think I'd better tell you the whole story.'

'Yes,' she replied quietly. 'Yes, I think perhaps you should.'

He leaned back in his chair and sighed deeply.

'It really all began when Mr Bennett and I were given her address to go along and value some stuff she wanted to sell. I wasn't very experienced then, but even so, I was appalled by the prices he was offering. His valuations were only a fraction of what I was sure her stuff was worth.

He shook his head, remembering how shocked he had been.

'It wasn't broken-down stuff either. No, it was beautiful — beautifully cared for and beautifully kept. The furniture had been polished until it shone like a mirror and every ornament was perfect.

'OK, so some of the pictures needed to be cleaned up a bit,' he conceded, 'but the frames were good and had been kept in good repair. Maybe they weren't paintings by the Old Masters — apparently those had to go when Thornpark was sold — but they were still very good paintings.

'I knew that all in all the stuff would bring in very good prices at auction.'

Susan sat back.

'You mean — you were buying the stuff, then re-selling it at auction on the firm's behalf, and not on Miss Mansfield's? I thought you were selling it for her, and the firm was taking a commission.'

Rex shook his head.

'No, sometimes Mortimer's likes to pick up antiques this way and pay for them with cash. Then the goods are put into auction later, sometimes after doing them up, and they fetch a much higher price.' He paused. 'It's fair enough if a lot of highly-skilled repair work has been done. But in Miss Mansfield's case — and between you and me, she isn't the only one — the pieces had been perfectly kept. They didn't need any mending, any stripping, or any re-polishing.

'Old Bennett was delighted with himself at doing such a good deal. In the car afterwards he began to tell me what he expected each piece to fetch at auction — and quite honestly, it made me sick to my stomach, especially since she's such a nice lady. She was so trusting. It felt like taking sweets from a child.'

'Oh, Rex!' Susan breathed. 'So what happened?'

'Well, I stewed on it for a bit — and then I got mad! I knew where I could get a proper price for Miss Mansfield's stuff, so I went back to the warehouse after we closed at the weekend, and I took it away with me. Only hers, I swear,' he said anxiously. 'No other stuff.'

'I believe you, Rex,' she assured him. 'So then what happened?'

'Well, then I took it to Fletcher's Antiques and let them see that I knew a thing or two about prices. We ended up doing a deal which was fair to both sides, and I took the money straight to Miss Mansfield.'

'Oh, Rex!' Susan said again, her eyes now shining with admiration. 'Was it a lot?'

'It was a good round figure.' He nodded. 'Enough to keep the wolf from the door for a while. Keep her warm, too. And buy her a new pair of shoes! I took her to buy those, and she chose the best. She's always been used to the best in shoes, has my Miss Mansfield,' he added proudly, and Susan could see how fond he had become of the old lady.

'And then — Mortimer's found out?' she guessed.

Rex laughed dryly.

'Old Bennett missed the goods in no time. They had been stored until the next auction, but he was walking home from work one evening for a change when he stopped to look in Fletcher's window. Of course he spotted one of the pieces straightaway, a distinctive fire screen which turns into a small desk at the turn of a hinge. A lovely neat little piece,' he added admiringly. 'Anyway, I was for it the next day.'

'Did you own up?' Susan asked.

Slowly Rex shook his head.

'I refused to make a statement,' he admitted.

Susan stared. 'But, Rex, you must! Surely it must count for something that you only sold Miss Mansfield's stuff, and that you gave her all the money?'

'How can I say anything?' he asked. 'They'd go and question her, and think how upset she'd be. She'd want to give it all back, and I'd have done it all for nothing.'

'Oh, Rex, I think it was a wonderful thing to do,' she breathed.

'Let's hope the enquiry thinks that way too!' he said ruefully. 'Oh, Susan, what can I say? I'll never get away with it. I really did help myself to that stuff.'

Susan shook her head, able at last to comprehend his dilemma.

'Anyway, I'm glad you know, darling,' he added. 'I'll get out of it somehow. And I'll get another job. Everything will come right. I feel I have a future now with you behind me, if only you'll say you'll marry me — as soon as possible.'

He gazed at her, his eyes full of hope, and reached out to take her hand. 'Say you will, Susan.'

She stared at him, hardly knowing what to say.

How much did she care for him now, she wondered. She had known for some time that the burning passion she had once felt for him had cooled considerably. But after hearing the real reason he was in trouble with his firm, she found she now had great warmth and respect for him.

He had done a very fine thing in trying to help old Miss Mansfield, and she applauded his efforts.

And yet . . . her thoughts went to Neil and her heart began to beat unevenly. He would soon receive her letter telling him all about her affair with Rex. How would he take the news? Would he feel that he didn't want to see her again? Would she mind so very much?

* * *

Rex watched the shadows chasing themselves across her face and he squeezed her fingers reassuringly.

'You want to wait until after the enquiry? That's it, isn't it? Well, perhaps that's sensible, darling. I could end up in awful disgrace, if not worse.'

'No, it's nothing to do with the enquiry,' she assured him hastily. 'Only, I really don't know how I feel these days, Rex. So much has happened. I don't know . . .'

He looked at her intently, then sat back and tried to force down his disappointment.

'Your mother said you were taking a job in Scotland,' he said, 'a job with Neil Faulkner's firm. Is that true?'

'It . . . it isn't settled,' she told him awkwardly.

She couldn't tell him about the letter she'd just posted to Neil.

They sat in silence for a while. Rex studied her downcast face. Had she fallen in love with this Neil Faulkner, he wondered. Had he fallen in love with her? The other man would certainly have more to offer her, he considered ruefully.

But Rex couldn't question her, and she obviously wasn't ready to confide in him.

For himself he was content to wait a little longer.

'Why not think about it?' he urged. 'We'll talk about it after everything's resolved. Will that do?'

'I think so,' she agreed hesitantly.

He leaned forward and kissed her, but she felt nothing more than the desire to weep.

'Come on, I'll take you home,' Rex told her. 'It'll all come right, you'll see,' he added reassuringly.

★ ★ ★

When Neil received Susan's letter he had to read it through twice before the import of the words struck deep into his heart. He couldn't pretend that it didn't hurt to know that Susan had had a passionate love for Rex Windham, and for a long time he sat in the study staring into space, hardly aware of his surroundings. So much so that Robert, who had come home much earlier than he'd anticipated, had to speak to him twice before he roused himself sufficiently to answer.

Robert was very tired, and as he slumped into a chair he mused that he was beginning to feel he was truly middle-aged for the first time since he'd passed his fiftieth birthday.

He felt that he was staring the destruction of all his dreams for himself and his family in the face.

Earlier that evening he'd visited Stella — the appointment they had previously arranged, the appointment that would seal his fate.

All day he'd been in torment,

wondering whether to discard his inhibitions and meet her desire for him with his for her.

When he left the office, he had finally persuaded himself to do it, and the decision seemed to lift a weight off his shoulders. Why shouldn't he and Stella have a closer relationship? It would take nothing from Laura, and in fact, she could benefit in the long run. He and Stella would work all the better together to increase the business.

He was almost light-hearted when he reached Stella's home and her enquiring look cleared magically as she greeted him.

'So you've decided to come to me after all, darling,' she said, her voice warm with satisfaction. 'I thought you would.'

Perhaps it was that smug air of satisfaction which had started the reversal of his decision, Robert considered as he leaned back in his favourite armchair in the study.

Or perhaps it was a sudden vision of

Laura as she'd been that morning when she'd poured him another cup of coffee and caught his hand as he reached for the cream.

'Can we talk sometime, Robert?' she'd asked. There had been a catch in her voice and her eyes had been anxious. 'Soon? Please?' she had added.

It would be holidays again, he'd thought tiredly. Then he'd looked at her as he'd nodded — and had suddenly noticed how fresh and well groomed she had looked.

How much did she see of David Croft, he wondered. It was harmless, of course; he had reassured himself on that point when they had all had dinner together. But he had formed the impression that Croft found Laura very attractive.

The image of her appealing face stayed with him for a long time during the day, but then he pushed her from his mind as the time came for him to talk to Stella Ross.

He had no more appetite for the

supper she had cooked than he'd had for Annie McCall's, but if Stella noticed, she chose not to comment. Once they had finished, she quickly cleared the dining-table and made coffee liqueurs for them to enjoy while they relaxed in front of the fire.

'What's it to be, Robert?' she asked without preamble. 'Or need I ask?'

'It seems I have no choice,' he told her bluntly. 'I need that lease, and I need it now.'

'Do I really need to bribe you with a lease on the Telefix building, Robert?' She sighed sadly. 'Am I so unattractive to you?'

'You know very well that you're very attractive to me, but . . .'

He didn't have a chance to finish his sentence as she slid into his arms, and then he was crushing her to him and kissing her passionately.

It was like many other evenings he had spent with Stella, but tonight was different. Tonight he wouldn't be allowed to hurry away.

Nor did he want to, thought Robert as he held her fragrant body in his arms. He could feel her desire for him, and his response was as great as her own.

Then, as though he were waking from a dream, he seemed to see Laura's clear eyes regarding him. How could he ever meet those eyes again if he let Stella win?

Besides, something in the faint air of triumph about her repelled him. She was so confident that she had beaten him in this struggle of wills, and it meant he would always be subservient to her in the future. And if he stayed with her now, he wouldn't have Laura's love to sustain him.

Laura's love! He stiffened in Stella's arms. For the first time in years the realisation hit him that he truly loved his wife.

He loved her. He loved his wife, and nothing was worth the risk of losing that love. But lose it he would if he went through with this madness.

Perhaps saying no to Stella would mean that they would lose Fernhurst, but if that was the price he had to pay for retaining his self-respect and his wife's love — well then, pay it he would. He could always find another house for them to make into a much-loved home.

Suddenly Robert pushed Stella away and smoothed back his hair.

'It's no use, Stella,' he told her unsteadily. 'Perhaps you win, but I'm afraid I lose.' He shrugged. 'If I lose Fernhurst, so be it — and if Neil can't get his business off the ground and loses everything he's put into it, then that's the way it has to be too.' He paused before saying with deliberation: 'But I can't let Laura down. I can't go on seeing you like this,' he added.

Stella's eyes glittered.

'Does Laura know we've been seeing one another?' she asked in a dangerously quiet voice.

'Frankly, I don't know and I don't care at this moment.'

'You're still in love with her,' she accused.

'What there is between my wife and me is entirely our affair,' Robert said quietly. 'I'm sorry. You can keep the Telefix lease, Stella. I'm tired of angling after it.'

'I think you're being very foolish, Robert,' she said lightly, though again there were sparks of anger in her eyes. She wasn't used to rejection. 'You know very well there's nowhere else.'

'Perhaps not, but I don't think I'm being foolish,' he told her as he stood up. 'Goodnight, Stella,' he said softly. 'I'm sorry it's had to end this way.'

She didn't reply and he let himself out into the cool evening air.

★　★　★

At home Robert found that Laura was out for the evening — something to do with the WI. Neil had arrived home earlier and was in the study reading his mail.

Robert walked into the room, knowing that he had to prepare Neil for the worst. It was time he knew exactly where he stood.

Neil looked up from reading Susan's letter — and the sight of his father's strained face drove everything else from his mind. Obviously there was something wrong.

'What's happened?' he asked, as Robert sank down heavily in his chair.

'You'd better know, Neil,' Robert said quietly, 'we can't have Telefix. I don't want to go into the details, but we can forget about moving in there.'

'But, Dad . . . ' Neil began, then bit his lip.

He wanted to ask a thousand questions but the look on his father's face forbade even one. An odd flash of intuition gave Neil a faint glimpse of the reason behind Stella Ross's refusal to grant them the lease.

'The price was too much to pay,' Robert said quietly, and Neil knew he wasn't referring to the financial deal.

For a long time they sat together in contemplative silence, then Neil came to put an arm round his father's shoulders.

'Thanks for all your efforts to help me, Dad,' he said. 'I . . . I just want to stay how much I appreciate it. Even though it's probably come to nothing . . . I'm proud that you thought me worthy of your support.'

Robert Faulkner nodded, gripping his son's hand, too afraid to speak in case he had no voice to say anything.

'But maybe we're not finished yet,' Neil went on, his eyes narrowing thoughtfully. 'If you don't mind, Dad, I'm going to go for a long walk and think about this. I won't be stuck for a job, you know. I do have contacts, and you . . . well, you're still a partner in Ross/Faulkner Industries.'

But would they have Fernhurst, Robert wondered. How long would the bank wait for them as they tried to clear up the financial mess? The loss would be heavy, both for him and Neil. But he felt proud of his son and managed to smile.

'That's the spirit, lad,' he said huskily.

* * *

Laura drove home from the WI meeting feeling tired and depressed. She still hadn't had a chance to talk to Robert.

No doubt he would be late home, as was usual these days, but tonight she intended to wait up for him. She must know what had gone wrong between them, even if it meant facing up to something she dared not even think about.

As she walked into the hall she saw that a light was on in the sitting-room, and walked straight through. No doubt Neil would be watching television. His trip to Edinburgh had been cancelled because of some sort of business hold-up, but Laura didn't know the details.

However, to her surprise it was Robert who rose to his feet and turned to look at her.

How smart she looked, he thought, his eyes travelling over her trim figure. He recognised the suit — but for the first time he noticed how she wore it with a natural elegance.

'Why, Robert!' she said. 'I didn't expect to see you. It's early yet. Shall I get you some coffee?'

'Sit down, Laura,' he said gravely, and something in his attitude struck fear in her heart. She had never seen him look so despondent.

'You'd better tell me about it,' she said quietly. 'I know there's something wrong, Robert. I . . . I've known for some time that things aren't . . . well, quite right between us.' She looked up at his closed, expressionless face. 'But — but if your feelings have changed, I'd rather know, although I can't promise . . . '

She broke off, feeling her throat constricting. Now that the time had come to clear the air between them, she knew she couldn't give him up.

'What are you talking about?' Robert was asking.

Laura ran her tongue over dry lips.

'I know very well that we're nothing to each other these days,' she began, 'and I'll understand if you don't love me any more. If, in fact, you've perhaps never loved me, Robert. I've often wondered if you only married me because of who I was . . . because you love Fernhurst so much.'

'Good grief!' Robert exclaimed. 'Fernhurst!'

'Does it mean so much to you?' she asked.

Suddenly, impulsively, he reached out and pulled her into his arms.

'It means everything to me because it's our home, Laura. *Our* home, yours and mine,' he said huskily. Then he gently loosened his hold on her. 'But I . . . may have lost it for us.'

Her eyes opened wide. 'Lost it? What do you mean?'

'I put it up as collateral for a loan at the bank to launch Neil's new project,' he told her. 'It required a great deal of capital, a sum I couldn't raise from Ross/Faulkner.'

Laura nodded but was obviously stunned.

'We needed premises and the Telefix building came available,' he continued in explanation, 'so I encouraged Neil to go for that and not to look for anywhere else.'

He sighed heavily. 'Stella Ross owns Telefix. She kept us waiting . . . until time eventually ran out. We can't meet the repayments, Laura. Oh, darling,' he said with desperation, 'I've lost Fernhurst for us.'

She stared at him. What could he be saying? How could they have lost Fernhurst? It didn't make sense.

'I don't believe it,' she said flatly. 'I don't believe you've lost our home. Can't you talk to Stella? Why can't she lease the building to you? I thought you and she . . . that you and she . . . '

She couldn't finish, and as she and Robert stared at one another, she began to understand.

'I couldn't pay the price, Laura,' he said in a low voice. 'I couldn't. I won't lie to you — I nearly did, but then I knew I couldn't betray you.'

'Oh, Robert!' she whispered, white to the lips.

His head went down in shame.

'I'm not proud of myself, Laura,' he said in a low voice. 'If you hate and despise me, it's only what I deserve.

'I've always felt that perhaps you . . . you didn't love me so very much when we married, but I knew you were grateful that you still lived in fernhurst. At least I've always been able to give you that because I know how much you love it.'

'Not more than I love you, Robert,' she told him. 'Fernhurst is my home — but you're my life. Oh, Robert, I'd never have let you go to Stella Ross.'

He was holding her very closely, his heart full of thankfulness. He didn't deserve her love, he told himself. How often had he failed to appreciate her, and even compared her to other women — women who couldn't hold a candle to her, he now acknowledged.

'I'll never rest until I get Fernhurst back for you,' he whispered fervently.

'Back for *us*,' she amended, 'if we want it. Perhaps it's time to move on, Robert. We aren't getting any younger.'

'We aren't all that old either,' he said, and sudden energy began to flow through him. 'You know, Neil was right. He said we shouldn't give up so easily — though dear only knows how I can get us out of this one! I can't even think straight these days.'

'It seems to me you're doing very well,' she said, smiling. Then she rose and took his hand. 'Come on, darling, let's go to bed.'

Together they mounted the stairs, as they had done so often in the past.

Picking Up The Pieces

Susan waited anxiously for a reply to her letter, but when none came she persuaded herself that it had been delayed in the post.

In the meantime, Rex had called to see her once or twice.

It was only five days now until the enquiry would be held over the sale of the goods from Mortimer's, and he would know then if there would be criminal proceedings. The thought made him sick with nerves.

On the following Friday Rex was busy in his flat when the telephone rang and he recognised the rather husky voice of old Mr Mortimer's secretary.

'Hello — Mr Windham?' she asked.

'Yes.' He could barely whisper the word.

'Could you possibly come along to Mr Mortimer's office?' she went on.

'Mr Mortimer — Senior, that is — would like to see you.'

'When would he like me to come?'

'Right now, Mr Windham, if you can. It's rather important and he'd like to speak to you personally.'

Rex glanced at his wristwatch.

'OK. I should be there in about ten minutes,' he judged.

He was there in twelve — the longest twelve minutes of his life as his thoughts teemed with questions. What did the old man want?

The secretary announced his arrival and asked him to go straight in, and a moment later Rex walked into the rather oppressive office with walls panelled in dark oak and a well-worn Turkish carpet on the floor.

Mr Mortimer was sitting behind his desk, but Rex stopped dead in his tracks as a tiny elderly lady rose from the seat opposite and turned to smile at him.

'Miss Mansfield!' He gasped. 'What are you doing here?'

'Hello, Mr Windham,' she said. 'Mr Mortimer and I have been having quite a chat.'

Rex found himself bereft of words as he turned to old Mr Mortimer, who regarded him steadily through a pair of thick, horn-rimmed spectacles.

'This is the young man you were telling me about, Miss Mansfield?' the old man confirmed.

'Oh yes, indeed, Mr Mortimer. This is Mr Windham.'

Miss Mansfield turned a pair of bright trusting eyes on Mr James Mortimer. Surely now he would understand all she had been trying to say. Surely she hadn't been wrong about Mr Windham.

She had been left feeling very puzzled after Susan had called to see her. For a start it hadn't escaped her notice that Susan had been taken aback when she had opened the door to her. The girl had been expecting a younger woman, Miss Mansfield had thought shrewdly afterwards.

She had also felt that only some sort of extreme anxiety would cause a young lady like Miss Ashley to call on her, a complete stranger, uninvited, and when she had learned that Mr Windham had been suspended from his job, her unease had increased.

It hadn't been so very difficult to put two and two together. Why would Miss Ashley have come along to see her unless Rex's suspension from his job somehow had something to do with her?

From there Miss Mansfield had decided that Susan must surely have come to reason with her on Mr Windham's behalf, and that it all must have something to do with the extra money the young man had obtained for her antiques.

Having considered this carefully from every angle, Miss Mansfield had decided she was on the right track, and had then set about formulating some way to put things right.

She recalled that she had once met

Mr Mortimer, many, many years ago when her father had come up to London and brought her along with him as a special treat.

She remembered him as a reasonable man, and it had seemed to her that they should have a chat together over this matter. Thus she had lost no time in making this appointment at his office.

Mr Mortimer had listened carefully to all she had to tell him, and then had asked his secretary to bring him some sort of report. This he had read very carefully while she had patiently waited.

Finally he had looked up.

'It would appear that the young man in question took your pieces from our warehouse and re-sold them elsewhere, Miss Mansfield. And I don't have to remind you that those pieces were the property of this firm . . . at the time that he sold them, that is.

'A full enquiry is to be held on Tuesday, when he will be given every opportunity to confirm or deny this. In fact, it seems to me that I shouldn't be discussing this matter with you at all.'

'But I insist that you do, Mr Mortimer,' she had said firmly. 'I have had a difficult journey to get here, and I would prefer to think that I haven't made the effort in vain.'

She had opened her old-fashioned handbag and taken out a neatly handwritten list.

'I've made a list of the pieces which the young man obtained and the prices originally offered at the first visit, together with the prices Mr Windham then gave to me. As you'll see, there's a quite remarkable difference,' she had added with some asperity. 'Don't you agree, Mr Mortimer?'

The elderly man had studied the figures, then asked his secretary to request that Mr Bennett should come to the office.

'I'm afraid he's out at the moment, Mr Mortimer,' she had informed him. 'If you remember that big estate near Oxford is being sold up and he's gone to supervise. Mr Harper is in his office though. Would you like to see him?'

'No, that won't be necessary. But could you telephone Mr Windham at home and ask him if he can possibly come in to see me right away?'

'Of course, sir.'

Now Mr Mortimer watched the door closing behind Rex. He knew Rex by sight and he had considered him a decent, responsible young man, but . . . Mr Mortimer pursed his lips. He applauded the young man's motives, but he certainly couldn't approve of his methods!

At the same time, he was going to have a word or two to say to his son Clive when he saw him, as well as Oliver Bennett. Just what had they been up to when his back was turned?

When Rex sat down next to Miss Mansfield, Mr Mortimer surveyed him carefully.

'So, Mr Windham, tell me about this situation you've got yourself into . . . '

'Have you got a receipt from Fletcher's?' he asked, after he'd listened to Rex's story, having practically had to drag it out of him; Rex didn't relish haven't to tell everything in front of Miss Mansfield, and he gave her several anxious glances.

'I have a receipt for everything,' he confirmed. He fumbled in his pocket for his wallet and extracted a slip of pink paper. 'Here it is, for the whole account.'

'Then you paid Miss Mansfield every penny?' Mr Mortimer said, having studied the receipt. 'You didn't keep any . . . ah . . . commission?'

'I wasn't entitled to commission,' Rex said.

Mr Mortimer sighed deeply.

'You have done wrong by the firm. You realise that, don't you? Where would we be if everyone took matters into their own hands — eh?' He looked sternly at Rex. 'Those pieces were not yours to sell, young man.'

'That's as may be,' Miss Mansfield put in, 'but I would suggest that if you are going to lecture this young man on the difference between right and wrong, the rest of your employees might benefit equally from it, while your firm might also bear further examination, Mr Mortimer. People in glass houses, and all that.' She smiled sweetly.

'One is inclined to trust Mortimer Antiques,' she continued. 'You have a certain reputation, you know, and one is inclined to accept a valuation as being the best possible because of that reputation. However, if your name should become tarnished because of some less than scrupulous business dealings . . . ' Again she smiled sweetly but there was a glint of steel in her eye.

'Er . . . quite,' Mr Mortimer agreed, and darted an uncomfortable glance at the old lady.

'I think we can drop this enquiry,' he went on, turning to Rex, 'but I also think it would be unwise to reinstate you in the firm, Windham. However — ' he went on quickly, as he saw Miss Mansfield open her mouth to object ' — I happen to know of a vacancy in another firm.

'I could arrange an interview for you — though they would have to know what has happened here, of course. However, if something can be arranged, I suggest that in the future you behave in a more circumspect fashion with regard to anything which is purchased on behalf of your firm. If you disagree with a valuation, then you must consult your superiors, not simply take matters into your own hands. Is that clear?'

'Very clear. Thank you, sir.'

Rex's eyes began to shine. If only he *could* make a new start!

'I think we've all learned our lesson, Mr Mortimer,' Miss Mansfield was saying clearly in her bell-like voice. 'But thank you for your attention,' she added, rising to her feet.

The older man stared at her, then also rose to his feet.

'We've been fortunate to have such expert guidance, ma'am,' he said, smiling. 'I promise you it won't happen again.'

Rex was happy to escort Miss Mansfield back home. He felt wonderful now that the great heavy cloud of uncertainty had been lifted from his shoulders, and instead of having to face an enquiry at which he had felt he would have nothing to say, he was going to be given an interview for a new job.

'I'll really work hard there,' he told Miss Mansfield. 'If I get the job, that is.'

'You must leave that to Mr Mortimer. He can't accuse you without accusing himself. However, now that that's all over, why don't you bring that nice young lady to tea on Sunday?'

'Thank you.' Rex accepted gratefully. 'I'm sure we'll both enjoy that.'

'Is there a romance?' the old lady asked, her old eyes twinkling with kindly interest.

Rex sobered. Was there a romance? Sadly he was beginning to doubt it.

'Perhaps there is . . . but not with me,' he added ruefully.

Miss Mansfield gazed at him, her eyes gentle with understanding.

'One can learn to be happy alone,' she said softly, then smiled as she squeezed his arm, 'but I'm sure a young man like you won't be alone for long.'

★ ★ ★

Neil had hesitated before writing to Susan. So much in his life seemed to hang in the balance right now that he hardly knew how he was going to proceed.

His whole mind had to be so focussed on making plans to save his new firm and to finding temporary premises that he had deliberately tried to put her letter to one side. But he was beginning to realise what a compliment she had paid him by telling him everything about her past affair.

Why had she told him? He could only assume it was because he had become important to her, as she was to him.

But he needed some sort of future to offer her. How could he ask her to share his life if it was full of doubts and potential failure?

As he sat alone at home on Saturday evening — his parents had gone out to dinner at their favourite restaurant — he could stand the uncertainty no longer.

He was sure that he still had some fight in him, but he couldn't do anything without Susan by his side. He had to know how he stood.

Picking up the phone, Neil dialled the Ashleys' London home . . .

It was Mr Ashley who answered.

'I'm afraid Susan isn't here at the moment,' he explained. 'But I'll get her to ring you as soon as she comes in, if you like.'

'Yes, please,' Neil said fervently.

★ ★ ★

An hour later the phone rang and Neil leapt to his feet to snatch it up.

'Susan?' he asked eagerly.

'No, it's Stella Ross,' a crisp voice

said in his hear. 'May I speak to your father, please, Neil?'

'I'm afraid he's out at the moment,' Neil told her.

'Then I'll ring later. But you can tell him I've finally made up my mind about the Telefix lease.'

Having expected to hear Susan's voice on the line, Neil was slightly disconcerted to hear Stella Ross. Then, suddenly, when she mentioned Telefix, his thoughts became crystal clear.

'I'll certainly give my father your message, Miss Ross,' he told her, 'but if you're ringing about the Telefix lease, you should talk to me. After all, the application for that lease refers to my firm, not my father's.'

It was Stella's turn to be disconcerted.

'Oh! Oh — well, then, I've decided that you can have the building after all, Neil. I've changed my mind about retaining it. You can have it.'

Neil thought quickly.

'That's very kind of you — but I'm not sure that I need it now,' he said coolly. 'You see, when you were so dilatory about leasing it to me, I decided to make other plans.'

'What do you mean?' Her voice grew sharp. 'You know there's nowhere else at all suitable for you in this whole area.'

'Ah, but there's nothing in my rule book which says I must confine my business to this area, Miss Ross. But, of course, I can quite see why you've changed your mind. So few people are willing to set up new businesses these days, especially a business for which that building would be suitable.' He looked as though he was considering. 'I can see that you might find it really quite difficult to lease it — and your terms would have to be outstanding.'

'The terms of lease have already been negotiated, Neil,' she put in crisply.

'But not accepted, Stella,' he returned pleasantly, but with a thread of steel running through his voice. 'As I say, it's required for my business, not my father's.'

There was a silence.

'Anyway, my parents have gone out for the evening,' he went on, 'but I'll ask my father to contact you as soon as he comes in — though they may be very late. Perhaps tomorrow would be better. Goodnight then, Stella — '

'Neil, wait . . . ' He could hear her breathing rather deeply. 'Look, the lease only requires my signature now — but perhaps I could alter the figures a little to accommodate you.'

'That's an interesting proposition, Stella. How much is a little?' Neil asked.

He was very cool as he negotiated the new figure, then, the deal complete, Stella suddenly laughed softly in his ear, and he could well understand his father's attraction to her.

'I always thought you were more like your mother, Neil, and not quite a businessman. I was wrong. But you're not like your father either,' she added. 'You're even more single-minded than him when you go after something you want.

'You're a hard man to deal with, Neil Faulkner, but maybe we can get together and do business once you're launched. As a matter of fact, I have a number of contacts who'd be very interested in your merchandise.'

'Maybe we can talk business, Stella,' he agreed pleasantly. 'I'll want that contract, though, when I call to see you tomorrow at nine-thirty. That should allow time for the figures to be adjusted.'

★ ★ ★

Once Stella had hung up, Neil wiped his forehead and poured himself a drink. What had got into him? Yet he knew that had probably been the first of many tests in his business life, and elation swept over him as he relished his evident success. He could do it!

The telephone rang again, and this time it *was* Susan.

'Neil?' she asked, and he could hear the uncertainty in her voice. 'Neil? Did you get my letter?'

'I did,' he told her.

There was a hesitation. He could hear her breathing.

'And?' she finally asked.

'It doesn't matter in the least.' His voice rang with confidence. 'That was part of your life before we met. All that belongs to you, and I don't think you should regret a moment of it. It's part of the girl I fell in love with, part of her warmth, and her generosity.'

Now he had heard her voice again, he couldn't hide his feelings for her.

'I need you so much, my darling,' he told her softly. 'I'm asking you to take on a marathon task, though — as my wife, not my secretary. I love you, Susan. I've loved you since the first moment I saw you. I want you by my side always. I'm asking you to marry me, darling.'

'Oh, Neil.' Susan's voice grew husky with tears of happiness. 'Of course I will. I love you, too, and I'll work with you in whatever way I can.'

'It won't be easy, darling,' Neil said. 'We're off to a late start, and I won't have much to offer you to begin with.'

'As if that matters!'

★   ★   ★

A little later Mr Ashley looked at the time and shook his head ruefully over the telephone bill he would be facing. But he had overheard enough to cause him to go into the sitting-room and quietly close the door, leaving Susan to her privacy in the hall.

Later he found a bottle of his special wine as a starry-eyed Susan put down a rather warm telephone receiver and rushed into the sitting room to breathlessly tell her parents: 'I'm going to marry Neil! He's just asked me and I said yes!'

They hugged her warmly, and she was almost knocked over by the exuberant Debbie.

'I thought it was Rex!' Debbie cried. 'Oh, this is terrific! I've always wanted a sister. Just wait till Mum hears. She'll be so thrilled. And Dad!'

And Dad! For the first time Susan felt a stab of dismay. How would Robert Faulkner view this?

However, when Neil's parents phoned later to wish her every happiness — Neil having broken the news to them as soon as went off the phone — Mr Faulkner's congratulations were every bit as warm as his wife's.

'I was wrong, Susan, about you and Neil, and I'm happy to admit it. You're good for him, my dear. A man needs a fine woman at his back. Just ask his mother!'

'Thank you, Mr Faulkner,' she said simply.

'If no-one else needs that telephone, I think I'll take it off the hook,' Mr Ashley joked later. 'It's high time we all went to bed.'

Happy Endings

The following Sunday Susan attended a celebration of a different kind when she and Rex went along to have tea with Miss Mansfield.

It had only taken one look at Susan's eyes for him to know that she had found true happiness with Neil Faulkner. Even in the days when they had been wildly in love, she hadn't looked like that. It was as though she was lit from within, and her face glowed with happiness when he called to collect her.

'I've got something to tell you, Rex,' she began, but he smiled at her, and put out his hand to take hers. His own disappointment was keen, but he would cope with that later.

'No need to say a word,' he told her. 'It's written all over you. It's Neil Faulkner, isn't it?'

She nodded.

'I tried not to fall in love with him,' she said. 'I didn't think it would work out — but it has and — oh, Rex, I'm so happy!' she burst out, unable to contain her joy.

'I'm thrilled for you, really I am,' he told her. 'And I can always settle for your rival.'

'My rival?'

His eyes twinkled.

'Miss Mansfield. Now if she were only sixty years younger . . . '

It was a very happy tea party. Susan had been greatly intrigued to hear all about the old lady's part in clearing up matters for Rex, and she happily listened to more of the story as she sat sipping tea once more out of the delicately fluted bone china cups.

'It was very naughty of you, Mr Windham,' Miss Mansfield was saying, 'risking your whole career like that, though I can never fully express my gratitude. But you must promise to consider things more carefully in your new job.'

'If I get it!' Rex pointed out. He was due to go for his interview on Wednesday.

'You'll get it,' Miss Mansfield assured him confidently. She was sure that Mr Mortimer would not have arranged it if he didn't expect the other firm to engage Rex.

She turned to Susan.

'And you, my dear, I hope you'll be very happy in your new life in Scotland. I hope Mr Windham will pass on news of you from time to time.'

'I'm going to see her off at the station tomorrow,' Rex said, 'and I'll expect an invitation to the wedding.'

'You'll both get an invitation to my wedding,' Susan assured them, her eyes sparkling. 'Mum and Debbie are going to have a fine old time organising it, though I expect Neil's mum will also have something to say.'

As they walked home they passed the fine window display of Fletcher's Antiques, the great rival to Mortimer's, and both stopped to gaze into the window.

As he surveyed the goods displayed there, Rex began to feel a familiar tingling in his fingers. He loved antiques. He had an affinity for these beautiful objects made by skilled craftsmen from a bygone age. How he had missed it all while he was suspended from his job.

He didn't know if the new firm would employ him or not, but he intended to try very hard indeed to make a new beginning.

'I might even work in Fletcher's one day,' he told Susan confidently. 'Yes, I might even work here.'

She smiled and took his arm as they crossed the street.

'If that's what you want, then I'm sure you will. I think you can do anything you put your mind to!'

★   ★   ★

It was Rex who came for Susan and escorted her to the station to see her off on the Scottish train. Both Mr Ashley and Debbie were at work, and Susan preferred to say goodbye to her mother at home.

Susan and Neil, together with his parents, would be back in a few weeks for the wedding, but even so, Helen Ashley was parting with her daughter yet again and it made her a little sad at heart.

However, as she looked at the glowing girl, she thanked God that she was so well now. Susan was certainly a different figure from the pale, anxious young woman who had travelled to Scotland several weeks before.

Rex was quiet as he saw to it that she had all her belongings with her, including the magazine and fruit he'd bought her to help make her journey more comfortable.

Her eyes misted at his kindness.

'Thank you, Rex.'

He stood on the platform for a long time after the train had left the station, then finally turned away. He would never forget Susan, but now a new and challenging future beckoned.

As the miles flew past, Susan's thoughts leapt ahead to the end of her journey, which in turn seemed to her to be the beginning of a new journey through life with Neil.

He had left her under no illusions as to how tough things were going to be, but she welcomed that. If they worked hard together, it would give them a strong, firm base for the rest of their lives. They would be well equipped to share everything, the successes as well as the failures.

Her head was full of dreams as the train pulled in at Lockerbie Station where Neil was waiting to meet her. It was so like, and yet so different from, the first time they had met that she almost felt she had stepped back in time.

But the young man who stepped forward to meet her was holding his arms wide, and Susan flew into his embrace.

And as Neil held her close and their lips met, she knew she had come home at last.

We do hope that you have enjoyed reading this large print book.

Did you know that all of our titles are available for purchase?

We publish a wide range of high quality large print books including:
Romances, Mysteries, Classics
General Fiction
Non Fiction and Westerns

Special interest titles available in large print are:
The Little Oxford Dictionary
Music Book, Song Book
Hymn Book, Service Book

Also available from us courtesy of Oxford University Press:
Young Readers' Dictionary
(large print edition)
Young Readers' Thesaurus
(large print edition)

For further information or a free brochure, please contact us at:
Ulverscroft Large Print Books Ltd.,
The Green, Bradgate Road, Anstey,
Leicester, LE7 7FU, England.
Tel: (00 44) **0116 236 4325**
Fax: (00 44) **0116 234 0205**

CHRISTMAS CHARADE

Kay Gregory

When Nina Petrov meets charismatic businessman Fenton Hardwick on a transcontinental train to Chicago, she sees him as the solution to her recurring Christmas problem. Every year her matchmaking father produces a different hopelessly unsuitable man for her to marry. Nina decides she needs a temporary fiancé to get him off her case, and Fen seems the perfect candidate for the job — until she makes the mistake of trying to pay him for his help . . .

A LETTER TO MY LOVE

Toni Anders

Devastated when Marcus married someone else, Sorrel resolved to devote her life to her toyshop and her invalid cousin, Alyse. However, when she meets Carl, the Bavarian woodcarver, it provides a romantic distraction — but Marcus's growing friendship with Alyse unsettles Sorrel. She is torn between her still-present love for Marcus, and her cousin's happiness. When Marcus's spiteful sister, Pamela, decides to repossess the toyshop for a wine bar, Sorrel decides to fight them both.

DOCTOR, DOCTOR

Chrissie Loveday

The arrival of a new doctor in a small Cornish hospital causes a stir, especially among the female members of staff. Lauren has worked hard to build her career, along with a protective shell to keep her emotions intact. She won't risk being hurt again, but Tom has other ideas . . . As they share the highs and lows of hospital life, they develop a mutual respect for each other's professional skills — but can there ever be more to their relationship?

YOURS FOR ETERNITY

Janet Whitehead

Danielle McMasters was haunted by the memory of the man she had loved and lost in a fatal car crash six years before. Ben was dead. So who, then, was the man watching her from across the room? His likeness was uncanny — it had to be Ben . . . hadn't it? But how could he have returned from the grave — and why was someone following her every move? The past was haunting her present, but how would it affect her future?